The Adventures
of
PINOCCHIO

The Adventures of

PINOCCHIO

by C. Collodi

translated from the Italian by
CAROL DELLA CHIESA

illustrated by
ATTILIO MUSSINO

MACMILLAN PUBLISHING COMPANY
New York
COLLIER MACMILLAN PUBLISHERS
London

Copyright © 1969 by Macmillan Publishing Company,
a division of Macmillan, Inc.
Illustrations © by Giunti Marzocco S.P.A., Firenze
All rights reserved. No part of this book may be reproduced
or transmitted in any form or by any means, electronic or
mechanical, including photocopying, recording, or by any
information storage and retrieval system, without
permission in writing from the Publisher.
Macmillan Publishing Company
866 Third Avenue, New York, NY 10022
Collier Macmillan Canada, Inc.
Printed and bound in Italy
First American Edition 1925; reissued 1969; reissued 1989

10   9   8   7   6   5   4   3   2   1

Library of Congress Cataloging-in-Publication Data
Collodi, Carlo, 1826-1890.
The adventures of Pinocchio.
Translation of: Avventure di Pinocchio.
Summary: A wooden puppet full of tricks and mischief,
with a talent for getting into and out of trouble,
wants more than anything else to become a real boy.
[1. Fairy tales. 2. Puppets—Fiction]
I. Della Chiesa, Carol, 1887–   . II. Mussino,
Attilio, ill. III. Title.
PZ8.L887Ad 1989   [Fic]   88-26684
ISBN 0-02-722821-5

FOREWORD

I think I'll call him Pinocchio. This name will make his fortune. I knew a whole family of Pinocchi once—Pinocchio the father, Pinocchia the mother, and Pinocchi the children—and they were all lucky. The richest of them begged for his living.

Geppetto said this to himself as he began to carve the Marionette. Whether his name had anything to do with it or not, Pinocchio was even luckier. He sprang out of the imagination of C. Collodi (the pen name of Carlo Lorenzini) and became a favorite of children at once.

It started in 1881 when the first chapter of *La storia di un burratino* (as it was then called) appeared in the July 7th issue of a weekly paper for children, *Giornale per i bambini*. The warmth of the reception could have come from sheer delight in the tale. But its deeply Italian character must have tinged the quick response. After all, Italy had just been united. And here was a story imbued with the spirit of Italian life. Pinocchio was the embodiment of Italian boyhood, capricious and mischievous but at the same time tender and loving. His adventures are like scenes in the *commedie dell'arte,* where tears and laughter come together, where the play of human feelings underlies the surface of masks and slapstick.

There have been many illustrated editions of *Pinocchio.* Even the first illustrations, the line drawings by an anonymous artist in the *Giornale,* caught something of Pinocchio's spirit. And Eugenio Mazzanti who illustrated the admirable first edition (1883) was somewhat indebted to that first artist. Carlo Chiostri who illustrated the second edition, in turn, owed something to Mazzanti. But it was not until the first large edition with illustrations by Attilio Mussino (1911) that the book came into flower. In his introduction to that edition Mussino bowed graciously to Mazzanti and Chiostri, and then to Pinocchio himself who possessed his imagination during the entire year he spent on the drawings. He transformed the book into a large picture book with page after page of pictures equally matched with the text in verve, color and incident. One can almost get the movement of the story from the pictures without reading it.

The Macmillan Company made us all its debtors in 1925 by publishing an American edition in the same format with the same Mussino drawings, and a new translation by Carol Della Chiesa. A generation of American children were able to enjoy this edition until it went out of print.

It is a pleasure to welcome it back, somewhat refurbished, in the same format as the new Italian edition published last year. Some pages have been redesigned, some drawings enlarged, some colors altered, but Mussino's spirit still pervades the book. They are all there as before: the familiar perky profile of Pinocchio, his paper clothes, his bread hat, and his friends good and bad — Geppetto, Master Cherry, the Cat and the Fox, the Carabineers, the Green Fisherman, Fire Eater, the Blue Fairy, and the rest. *Evviva!*

Maria Cimino

Chilmark, Massachusetts
September 1968

CONTENTS

CHAPTER 1

How it happened that Mastro Cherry, carpenter, found a piece of wood that wept and laughed like a child.

Centuries ago there lived—

"A king!" my little readers will say immediately.

No, children, you are mistaken. Once upon a time there was a piece of wood. It was not an expensive piece of wood. Far from it. Just a common block of firewood, one of those thick, solid logs that are put on the fire in winter to make cold rooms cozy and warm.

I do not know how this really happened, yet the fact remains that one fine day this piece of wood found itself in the shop of an old carpenter. His real name was Mastro Antonio, but everyone called him Mastro Cherry, for the tip of his nose was so round and red and shiny that it looked like a ripe cherry.

As soon as he saw that piece of wood, Mastro Cherry was filled

with joy. Rubbing his hands together happily, he mumbled half to himself:

"This has come in the nick of time. I shall use it to make the leg of a table."

He grasped the hatchet quickly to peel off the bark and shape the wood. But as he was about to give it the first blow, he stood still with arm uplifted, for he had heard a wee, little voice say in a beseeching tone: "Please be careful! Do not hit me so hard!"

What a look of surprise shone on Mastro Cherry's face! His funny face became still funnier.

He turned frightened eyes about the room to find out where that wee, little voice had come from and he saw no one! He looked under the bench—no one! He peeped inside the closet—no one! He searched among the shavings—no one! He opened the door to look up and down the street—and still no one!

"Oh, I see!" he then said, laughing and scratching his wig. "It can easily be seen that I only thought I heard the tiny voice say the words! Well, well—to work once more."

He struck a most solemn blow upon the piece of wood.

"Oh, oh! You hurt!" cried the same far-away little voice.

Mastro Cherry grew dumb, his eyes popped out of his head, his mouth opened wide, and his tongue hung down on his chin.

As soon as he regained the use of his senses, he said, trembling and stuttering from fright:

"Where did that voice come from, when there is no one around? Might it be that this piece of wood has learned to weep and cry like a child? I can hardly believe it. Here it is—a piece of common firewood, good only to burn in the stove, the same as any other. Yet—might someone be hidden in it? If so, the worse for him. I'll fix him."

With these words, he grabbed the log with both hands and started to knock it about unmercifully. He threw it to the floor, against the walls of the room, and even up to the ceiling.

He listened for the tiny voice to moan and cry. He waited

two minutes—nothing; five minutes—nothing; ten minutes—nothing.

"Oh, I see," he said, trying bravely to laugh and ruffling up his wig with his hand. "It can easily be seen I only imagined I heard the tiny voice! Well, well—to work once more!"

The poor fellow was scared half to death, so he tried to sing a gay song in order to gain courage.

He set aside the hatchet and picked up the plane to make

the wood smooth and even, but as he drew it to and fro, he heard the same tiny voice. This time it giggled as it spoke:

"Stop it! Oh, stop it! Ha, ha, ha! You tickle my stomach."

This time poor Mastro Cherry fell as if shot. When he opened his eyes, he found himself sitting on the floor.

His face had changed; fright had turned even the tip of his nose from red to deepest purple.

CHAPTER 2

Mastro Cherry gives the piece of wood to his friend Geppetto, who takes it to make himself a Marionette that will dance, fence, and turn somersaults.

In that very instant, a loud knock sounded on the door.

"Come in," said the carpenter, not having an atom of strength left with which to stand up.

At the words, the door opened and a dapper little old man came in. His name was Geppetto, but to the boys of the neighborhood he was Polendina [Cornmeal Mush], on account of the wig he always wore which was just the color of yellow corn.

Geppetto had a very bad temper. Woe to the one who called him Polendina! He became as wild as a beast and no one could soothe him.

"Good day, Mastro Antonio," said Geppetto. "What are you doing on the floor?"

"I am teaching the ants their A B C's."

"Good luck to you!"

"What brought you here, friend Geppetto?"

"My legs. And it may flatter you to know, Mastro Antonio, that I have come to you to beg for a favor."

"Here I am, at your service," answered the carpenter, raising himself onto his knees.

"This morning a fine idea came to me."

"Let's hear it."

"I thought of making myself a beautiful wooden Marionette. It must be wonderful, one that will be able to dance, fence, and turn somersaults. With it I intend to go around the world, to earn my crust of bread and cup of wine. What do you think of it?"

"Bravo, Polendina!" cried the same tiny voice which came from no one knew where.

On hearing himself called Polendina, Mastro Geppetto turned the color of a red pepper and, facing the carpenter, said to him angrily:

"Why do you insult me?"

"Who is insulting you?"

"You called me Polendina."

"I did not."

"I suppose you think *I* did! Yet I *know* it was you."

"No!"

"Yes!"

"No!"

"Yes!"

And growing angrier each moment, they went from words to blows, and finally began to scratch and bite and slap each other.

When the fight was over, Mastro Antonio had Geppetto's yellow wig in his hands and Geppetto found the carpenter's curly wig in his mouth.

"Give me back my wig!" shouted Mastro Antonio in a surly voice.

"You return mine and we'll be friends."

The two little old men, each with his own wig back on his own

head, shook hands and swore to be good friends for the rest of their lives.

"Well then, Mastro Geppetto," said the carpenter, to show he bore him no ill will, "what is it you want?"

"I want a piece of wood to make a Marionette. Will you give it to me?"

Mastro Antonio, very glad indeed, went immediately to his bench to get the piece of wood which had frightened him so much. But as he was about to give it to his friend, with a violent jerk it slipped out of his hands and hit against poor Geppetto's thin legs.

"Ah! Is this the gentle way, Mastro Antonio, in which you make your gifts? You have made me almost lame!"

"I swear to you I did not do it!"

"It was *I*, of course!"

"It's the fault of this piece of wood."

"You're right; but remember you were the one to throw it at my legs."

"I did not throw it!"

"Liar!"

"Geppetto, do not insult me or I shall call you Polendina."

"Idiot."

"Polendina!"

"Donkey!"

"Polendina!"

"Ugly monkey!"

"Polendina!"

On hearing himself called Polendina for the third time, Geppetto lost his head with rage and threw himself upon the carpenter. Then and there they gave each other a sound thrashing.

After this fight, Mastro Antonio had two more scratches on his nose, and Geppetto had two buttons missing from his coat. Thus having settled their accounts, they shook hands and swore to be good friends for the rest of their lives.

Then Geppetto took the fine piece of wood, thanked Mastro Antonio, and limped away toward home.

CHAPTER 3

*As soon as he gets home, Gep-
petto fashions the Marionette
and calls it Pinocchio. The
first pranks of the Marionette.*

Little as Geppetto's house was, it was neat and comfortable. It was a small room on the ground floor, with a tiny window under the stairway. The furniture could not have been much simpler: a very old chair, a rickety old bed, and a tumble-down table. A fireplace full of burning logs was painted on the wall opposite the door. Over the fire, there was painted a pot full of something which kept boiling happily away and sending up clouds of what looked like real steam.

As soon as he reached home, Geppetto took his tools and began to cut and shape the wood into a Marionette.

"What shall I call him?" he said to himself. "I think I'll call him Pinocchio [Pine Seed]. This name will make his fortune. I knew a whole family of Pinocchi once—Pinocchio the father, Pinocchia the mother, and Pinocchi the children—and they were all lucky. The richest of them begged for his living."

After choosing the name for his Marionette, Geppetto set seriously to work to make the hair, the forehead, the eyes. Fancy his surprise when he noticed that these eyes moved and then stared fixedly at him. Geppetto, seeing this, felt insulted and said in a grieved tone:

"Ugly wooden eyes, why do you stare so?"

There was no answer.

After the eyes, Geppetto made the nose, which began to stretch as soon as finished. It stretched and stretched and stretched till it became so long, it seemed endless.

Poor Geppetto kept cutting it and cutting it, but the more he cut, the longer grew that impertinent nose. In despair he let it alone.

Next he made the mouth.

No sooner was it finished than it began to laugh and poke fun at him.

"Stop laughing!" said Geppetto angrily; but he might as well have spoken to the wall.

"Stop laughing, I say!" he roared in a voice of thunder.

The mouth stopped laughing, but it stuck out a long tongue.

Not wishing to start an argument, Geppetto made believe he saw nothing and went on with his work.

After the mouth, he made the chin, then the neck, the shoulders, the stomach, the arms, and the hands.

As he was about to put the last touches on the finger tips, Geppetto felt his wig being pulled off. He glanced up and what did he see? His yellow wig was in the Marionette's hand. "Pinocchio, give me my wig!"

But instead of giving it back, Pinocchio put it on his own head, which was half swallowed up in it.

At that unexpected trick, Geppetto became very sad and downcast, more so than he had ever been before.

"Pinocchio, you wicked boy!" he cried out. "You are not yet finished, and you start out by

21

being impudent to your poor old father. Very bad, my son, very bad!"

And he wiped away a tear.

The legs and feet still had to be made. As soon as they were done, Geppetto felt a sharp kick on the tip of his nose.

"I deserve it!" he said to himself. "I should have thought of this before I made him. Now it's too late!"

He took hold of the Marionette under the arms and put him on the floor to teach him to walk.

Pinocchio's legs were so stiff that he could not move them, and Geppetto held his hand and showed him how to put out one foot after the other.

When his legs were limbered up, Pinocchio started walking by himself and ran all around the room. He came to the open door, and with one leap he was out into the street. Away he flew!

Poor Geppetto ran after him but was unable to catch him, for Pinocchio ran in leaps and bounds, his two wooden feet, as they beat on the stones of the street, making as much noise as twenty peasants in wooden shoes.

"Catch him! Catch him!" Geppetto kept shouting. But the people in the street, seeing a wooden Marionette running like the wind, stood still to stare and to laugh until they cried.

At last, by sheer luck, a Carabineer [a military policeman] happened along, who, hearing all that noise, thought that it might be a runaway colt, and stood bravely in the middle of the street, with legs wide apart, firmly resolved to stop it and prevent any trouble.

Pinocchio saw the Carabineer from afar and tried his best to escape between the legs of the big fellow, but without success.

The Carabineer grabbed him by the nose (it was an extremely long one and seemed made on purpose for that very thing) and returned him to Mastro Geppetto.

The little old man wanted to pull Pinocchio's ears. Think how he felt when, upon searching for them, he discovered that he had forgotten to make them!

All he could do was to seize Pinocchio by the back of the neck and take him home. As he was doing so, he shook him two or three times and said to him angrily:

"We're going home now. When we get home, then we'll settle this matter!"

Pinocchio, on hearing this, threw himself on the ground and refused to take another step. One person after another gathered around the two.

Some said one thing, some another.

"Poor Marionette," called out

a man. "I am not surprised he doesn't want to go home. Geppetto, no doubt, will beat him unmercifully, he is so mean and cruel!"

"Geppetto looks like a good man," added another, "but with boys he's a real tyrant. If we leave that poor Marionette in his hands he may tear him to pieces!"

They said so much that, finally, the Carabineer ended matters by setting Pinocchio at liberty and dragging Geppetto to prison. The poor old fellow did not know how to defend himself, but wept and wailed like a child and said between his sobs:

"Ungrateful boy! To think I tried so hard to make you a well-behaved Marionette! I deserve it, however! I should have given the matter more thought."

What happened after this is an almost unbelievable story, but you may read it, dear children, in the chapters that follow.

CHAPTER 4

*The story of Pinocchio and
the Talking Cricket, in which
one sees that bad children
do not like to be corrected
by those who know more than
they do.*

Very little time did it take to get poor old Geppetto to prison.
In the meantime that rascal, Pinocchio, free now from the clutches
of the Carabineer, was running wildly across fields and meadows,
taking one short cut after another toward home. In his wild flight,
he leaped over brambles and bushes, and across brooks and ponds,
as if he were a goat or a hare chased by hounds.

On reaching home, he found the house door half open. He
slipped into the room, locked the door, and threw himself on
the floor, happy at his escape.

But his happiness lasted only a short time, for just then he heard
someone saying:

"Cri-cri-cri!"

"Who is calling me?" asked Pinocchio, greatly frightened.

"I am!"

Pinocchio turned and saw a large cricket crawling slowly up the wall.

"Tell me, Cricket, who are you?"

"I am the Talking Cricket and I have been living in this room for more than one hundred years."

"Today, however, this room is mine," said the Marionette, "and if you wish to do me a favor, get out now, and don't turn around even once."

"I refuse to leave this spot," answered the Cricket, "until I have told you a great truth."

"Tell it, then, and hurry."

"Woe to boys who refuse to obey their parents and run away from home! They will never be happy in this world, and when they are older they will be very sorry for it."

"Sing on, Cricket mine, as you please. What I know is that to-morrow, at dawn, I leave this place forever. If I stay here the same thing will happen to me which happens to all other boys and girls. They are sent to school, and whether they want to or not, they must study. As for me, let me tell you, I hate to study! It's much more fun, I think, to chase after butterflies, climb trees, and steal birds' nests."

"Poor little silly! Don't you know that if you go on like that, you will grow into a perfect donkey and that you'll be the laughing-stock of everyone?"

"Keep still, you ugly Cricket!" cried Pinocchio.

But the Cricket, who was a wise old philosopher, instead of being offended at Pinocchio's impudence, continued in the same tone:

"If you do not like going to school, why don't you at least learn a trade, so that you can earn an honest living?"

"Shall I tell you something?" asked Pinocchio, who was beginning to lose patience. "Of all the trades in the world, there is only one that really suits me."

"And what can that be?"

"That of eating, drinking, sleeping, playing, and wandering around from morning till night."

"Let me tell you, for your own good, Pinocchio," said the Talking Cricket in his calm voice, "that those who follow that trade always end up in the hospital or in prison."

"Careful, ugly Cricket! If you make me angry, you'll be sorry!"

"Poor Pinocchio, I am sorry for you."

"Why?"

"Because you are a Marionette and, what is much worse, you have a wooden head."

At these last words, Pinocchio jumped up in a fury, took a hammer from the bench, and threw it with all his strength at the Talking Cricket.

Perhaps he did not think he would strike it. But, sad to relate, my dear children, he did hit the Cricket, straight on its head.

With a last weak "cri-cri-cri" the poor Cricket fell from the wall, dead!

CHAPTER 5

*Pinocchio is hungry
and looks for an egg
to cook himself an ome-
let; but, to his surprise,
the omelet flies out of
the window.*

If the Cricket's death scared Pinocchio at all, it was only for a very few moments. For, as night came on, a queer, empty feeling at the pit of his stomach reminded the Marionette that he had eaten nothing as yet.

A boy's appetite grows very fast, and in a few moments the queer, empty feeling had become hunger, and the hunger grew bigger and bigger, until soon he was as ravenous as a bear.

Poor Pinocchio ran to the fireplace where the pot was boiling and stretched out his hand to take the cover off, but to his amazement the pot was only painted! Think how he felt! His long nose became at least two inches longer.

He ran about the room, dug in all the boxes and drawers, and even looked under the bed in search of a piece of bread, hard though it might be, or a cooky, or perhaps a bit of fish. A bone left by a dog would have tasted good to him! But he found nothing.

And meanwhile his hunger grew and grew. The only relief poor Pinocchio had was to yawn; and he certainly did yawn, such a big yawn that his mouth stretched out to the tips of his ears. Soon he became dizzy and faint.

He wept and wailed to himself: "The Talking Cricket was right. It was wrong of me to disobey Father and to run away from home. If he were here now, I wouldn't be so hungry! Oh, how horrible it is to be hungry!"

Suddenly, he saw, among the sweepings in a corner, something round and white that looked very much like a hen's egg. In a jiffy he pounced upon it. It was an egg.

The Marionette's joy knew no bounds. It is impossible to describe it; you must picture it to yourself. Certain that he was dreaming, he turned the egg over and over in his hands, fondled it, kissed it, and talked to it:

"And now, how shall I cook you? Shall I make an omelet? No, it is better to fry you in a pan! Or shall I drink you? No, the best way is to fry you in a pan. You will taste better."

No sooner said than done. He placed a little pan over a foot warmer full of hot coals. In the pan, instead of oil or butter, he poured a little water. As soon as the water started to boil—tac!—he broke the eggshell. But in place of the white and the yolk of the egg, a little yellow Chick, fluffy and gay and smiling, escaped from it. Bowing politely to Pinocchio, he said to him:

"Many, many thanks, indeed, Mr. Pinocchio, for having saved me the trouble of breaking my shell! Good-by and

good luck to you and remember me to the family!"

With these words he spread out his wings and, darting to the open window, he flew away into space till he was out of sight.

The poor Marionette stood as if turned to stone, with wide eyes, open mouth, and the empty halves of the eggshell in his hands. When he came to himself, he began to cry and shriek at the top of his lungs, stamping his feet on the ground and wailing all the while:

"The Talking Cricket was right! If I had not run away from home and if Father were here now, I should not be dying of hunger. Oh, how horrible it is to be hungry!"

And as his stomach kept grumbling more than ever and he had nothing to quiet it with, he thought of going out for a walk to the near-by village, in the hope of finding some charitable person who might give him a bit of bread.

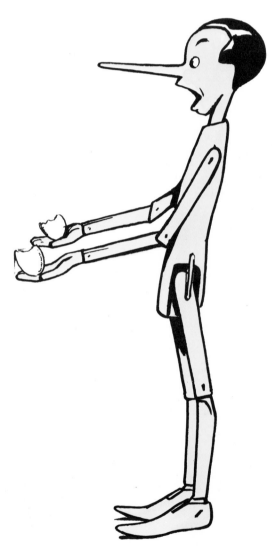

CHAPTER 6

Pinocchio falls asleep with his feet on a foot warmer, and awakens the next day with his feet all burned off.

Pinocchio hated the dark street, but he was so hungry that, in spite of it, he ran out of the house. The night was pitch black. It thundered, and bright flashes of lightning now and again shot across the sky, turning it into a sea of fire. An angry wind blew cold and raised dense clouds of dust, while the trees shook and moaned in a weird way.

Pinocchio was greatly afraid of thunder and lightning, but the hunger he felt was far greater than his fear. In a dozen leaps and bounds, he came to the village, tired out, puffing like a whale, and with tongue hanging.

The whole village was dark and deserted. The stores were closed, the doors, the windows. In the streets, not even a dog could be seen. It seemed the Village of the Dead.

Pinocchio, in desperation, ran up to a doorway, threw him-

self upon the bell and pulled it wildly, saying to himself:

"Someone will surely answer that!"

He was right. An old man in a nightcap opened the window and looked out. He called down angrily:

"What do you want at this hour of night?"

"Will you be good enough to give me a bit of bread? I am hungry."

"Wait a minute and I'll come right back," answered the old fellow, thinking he had to deal with one of those boys who love to roam around at night ringing people's bells while they are peacefully asleep.

After a minute or two, the same voice cried:

"Get under the window and hold out your hat!"

Pinocchio had no hat, but he managed to get under the window just in time to feel a shower of ice-cold water pour down on his poor wooden head, his shoulders, and over his whole body.

He returned home as wet as a rag, and tired out from weariness and hunger.

As he no longer had any strength left with which to stand, he sat down on a little stool and put his two feet on the stove to dry them.

There he fell asleep, and while he slept, his wooden feet began to burn. Slowly, very slowly, they blackened and turned to ashes.

Pinocchio snored away happily as if his feet were not his own. At dawn he opened his eyes just as a loud knocking sounded at the door.

"Who is it?" he called, yawning and rubbing his eyes.

"It is I," answered a voice.

It was the voice of Geppetto.

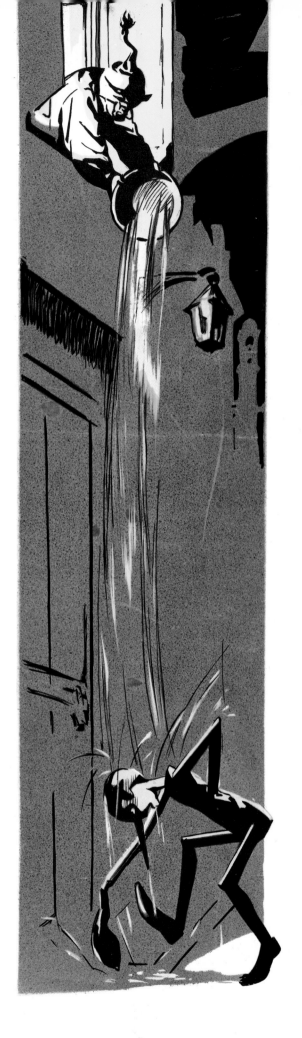

CHAPTER 7

*Geppetto returns home and
gives his own breakfast to
the Marionette.*

The poor Marionette, who was still half asleep, had not yet found out that his two feet were burned and gone. As soon as he heard his Father's voice, he jumped up from his seat to open the door, but, as he did so, he staggered and fell headlong to the floor.

In falling, he made as much noise as a sack of wood falling from the fifth story of a house.

"Open the door for me!" Geppetto shouted from the street.

"Father, dear Father, I can't," answered the Marionette in despair, crying and rolling on the floor.

"Why can't you?"

"Because someone has eaten my feet."

"And who has eaten them?"

"The cat," answered Pinocchio, seeing that little animal busily

playing with some shavings in the corner of the room.

"Open! I say," repeated Geppetto, "or I'll give you a sound whipping when I get in."

"Father, believe me, I can't stand up. Oh, dear! Oh, dear! I shall have to walk on my knees all my life."

Geppetto, thinking that all these tears and cries were only other pranks of the Marionette, climbed up the side of the house and went in through the window.

At first he was very angry, but on seeing Pinocchio stretched out on the floor and really without feet, he felt very sad and sorrowful. Picking him up from the floor, he fondled and caressed him, talking to him while the tears ran down his cheeks:

"My little Pinocchio, my dear little Pinocchio! How did you burn your feet?"

"I don't know, Father, but believe me, the night has been a terrible one and I shall remember it as long as I live. The thunder was so noisy and the lightning so bright—and I was hungry. And then the Talking Cricket said to me, 'You deserve it; you were bad'; and I said to him, 'Careful, Cricket'; and he said to me, 'You are a Marionette and you have a wooden head'; and I threw the hammer at him and killed him. It was his own fault, for I didn't want to kill him. And I put the pan on the coals, but the Chick flew away and said, 'I'll see you again! Remember me to the family.' And my hunger grew, and I went out, and the old man with a nightcap looked out of the window and threw water on me, and I came home and put my feet on the stove to dry them because I was still hungry, and I fell asleep and now my feet are gone but my hunger isn't! Oh!—Oh!—Oh!" And poor Pinocchio began to scream and cry so loudly that he could be heard for miles around.

Geppetto, who had understood nothing of all that jumbled talk, except that the Marionette was hungry, felt sorry for him, and pulling three pears out of his pocket, offered them to him, saying:

"These three pears were for my breakfast, but I give them to you gladly. Eat them and stop weeping."

"If you want me to eat them, please peel them for me."

"Peel them?" asked Geppetto, very much surprised. "I should never have thought, dear boy of mine, that you were so dainty and fussy about your food. Bad, very bad! In this world, even as children, we must accustom ourselves to eat of everything, for we never know what life may hold in store for us!"

"You may be right," answered Pinocchio, "but I will not eat the pears if they are not peeled. I don't like them."

And good old Geppetto took out a knife, peeled the three pears, and put the skins in a row on the table.

Pinocchio ate one pear in a twinkling and started to throw the core away, but Geppetto held his arm.

"Oh, no, don't throw it away! Everything in this world may be of some use!"

"But the core I will not eat!" cried Pinocchio in an angry tone.

"Who knows?" repeated Geppetto calmly.

And later the three cores were placed on the table next to the skins.

Pinocchio had eaten the three pears, or rather devoured them. Then he yawned deeply, and wailed:

"I'm still hungry."

"But I have no more to give you."

"Really, nothing—nothing?"

"I have only these three cores and these skins."

"Very well, then," said Pinocchio, "if there is nothing else I'll eat them."

At first he made a wry face, but, one after another, the skins and the cores disappeared.

"Ah! Now I feel fine!" he said after eating the last one.

"You see," observed Geppetto, "that I was right when I told you that one must not be too fussy and too dainty about food. My dear, we never know what life may have in store for us!"

CHAPTER 8

Geppetto makes Pin-
occhio a new pair
of feet, and sells his
coat to buy him an
A-B-C book.

The Marionette, as soon as his hunger was appeased, started to grumble and cry that he wanted a new pair of feet.

But Mastro Geppetto, in order to punish him for his mischief, let him alone the whole morning. After dinner he said to him:

"Why should I make your feet over again? To see you run away from home once more?"

"I promise you," answered the Marionette, sobbing, "that from now on I'll be good—"

"Boys always promise that when they want something," said Geppetto.

"I promise to go to school every day, to study, and to succeed—"

"Boys always sing that song when they want their own will."

"But I am not like other boys! I am better than all of them

and I always tell the truth. I promise you, Father, that I'll learn a trade, and I'll be the comfort and staff of your old age."

Geppetto, though trying to look very stern, felt his eyes fill with tears and his heart soften when he saw Pinocchio so unhappy. He said no more, but taking his tools and two pieces of wood, he set to work diligently.

In less than an hour the feet were finished, two slender, nimble little feet, strong and quick, modeled as if by an artist's hands.

"Close your eyes and sleep!" Geppetto then said to the Marionette.

Pinocchio closed his eyes and pretended to be asleep, while Geppetto stuck on the two feet with a bit of glue melted in an eggshell, doing his work so well that the joint could hardly be seen.

As soon as the Marionette felt his new feet, he gave one leap from the table and started to skip and jump around, as if he had lost his head from very joy.

"To show you how grateful I am to you, Father, I'll go to school now. But to go to school I need a suit of clothes."

Geppetto did not have a penny in his pocket, so he made his son a little suit of flowered paper, a pair of shoes from the bark of a tree, and a tiny cap from a bit of dough.

Pinocchio ran to look at himself in a bowl of water, and he felt so happy that he said proudly:

"Now I look like a gentleman."

"Truly," answered Geppetto. "But remember that fine clothes do not make the man unless they be neat and clean."

"Very true," answered Pinocchio, "but, in order to go to school, I still need something very important."

"What is it?"

"An A-B-C book."

"To be sure! But how shall we get it?"

"That's easy. We'll go to a bookstore and buy it."

"And the money?"

"I have none."

"Neither have I," said the old man sadly.

Pinocchio, although a happy boy always, became sad and downcast at these words. When

poverty shows itself, even mischievous boys understand what it means.

"What does it matter, after all?" cried Geppetto all at once, as he jumped up from his chair. Putting on his old coat, full of darns and patches, he ran out of the house without another word.

After a while he returned. In his hands he had the A-B-C book for his son, but the old coat was gone. The poor fellow was in his shirt sleeves and the day was cold.

"Where's your coat, Father?"

"I have sold it."

"Why did you sell your coat?"

"It was too warm."

Pinocchio understood the answer in a twinkling, and, unable to restrain his tears, he jumped on his father's neck and kissed him over and over.

CHAPTER 9

*Pinocchio sells his
A-B-C book to pay
his way into the
Marionette Theater.*

See Pinocchio hurrying off to school with his new A-B-C book under his arm! As he walked along, his brain was busy planning hundreds of wonderful things, building hundreds of castles in the air. Talking to himself, he said:

"In school today, I'll learn to read, tomorrow to write, and the day after tomorrow I'll do arithmetic. Then, clever as I am, I can earn a lot of money. With the very first pennies I make, I'll buy Father a new cloth coat. Cloth, did I say? No, it shall be of gold and silver with diamond buttons. That poor man certainly deserves it; for, after all, isn't he in his shirt sleeves because he was good enough to buy a book for me? On this cold day, too! Fathers are indeed good to their children!"

As he talked to himself, he thought he heard sounds of pipes and drums coming from a distance: pi-pi-pi, pi-pi-pi . . . zum, zum, zum, zum.

He stopped to listen. Those sounds came from a little street that led to a small village along the shore.

"What can that noise be? What a nuisance that I have to go to school! Otherwise . . . "

There he stopped, very much puzzled. He felt he had to make up his mind for either one thing or another. Should he go to school, or should he follow the pipes?

"Today I'll follow the pipes, and tomorrow I'll go to school. There's always plenty of time to go to school," decided the little rascal at last, shrugging his shoulders.

No sooner said than done. He started down the street, going like the wind. On he ran, and louder grew the sounds of pipe and drum: pi-pi-pi, pi-pi-pi, pi-pi-pi . . . zum, zum, zum, zum.

Suddenly, he found himself in a large square, full of people standing in front of a little wooden building painted in brilliant colors.

"What is that house?" Pinocchio asked a little boy near him.

"Read the sign and you'll know."

"I'd like to read, but somehow I can't today."

"Oh, really? Then I'll read it to you. Know, then, that written in letters of fire I see the words: 'Great Marionette Theater.'"

"When did the show start?"

"It is starting now."

"And how much does one pay to get in?"

"Four pennies."

Pinocchio, who was wild with curiosity to know what was going on inside, lost all his pride and said to the boy shamelessly:

"Will you give me four pennies until tomorrow?"

"I'd give them to you gladly," answered the other, poking fun at him, "but just now I can't give them to you."

"For the price of four pennies, I'll sell you my coat."

"If it rains, what shall I do with a coat of flowered paper? I could not take it off again."

"Do you want to buy my shoes?"

"They are only good enough to light a fire with."

"What about my hat?"

"Fine bargain, indeed! A cap of dough! The mice might come and eat it from my head!"

Pinocchio was almost in tears. He was just about to make one last offer, but he lacked the courage to do so. He hesitated, he wondered, he could not make up his mind. At last he said:

"Will you give me four pennies for the book?"

"I am a boy and I buy nothing from boys," said the little fellow with far more common sense than the Marionette.

"I'll give you four pennies for your A-B-C book," said a ragpicker who stood by.

Then and there, the book changed hands. And to think that poor old Geppetto sat at home in his shirt sleeves, shivering with cold, having sold his coat to buy that little book for his son!

CHAPTER 10

The Marionettes recognize their
brother Pinocchio, and greet
him with loud cheers; but the
Director, Fire Eater, happens
along and poor Pinocchio
almost loses his life.

Quick as a flash, Pinocchio disappeared into the Marionette Theater. And then something happened which almost caused a riot.

The curtain was up and the performance had started.

Harlequin and Pulcinella were reciting on the stage and, as usual, they were threatening each other with sticks and blows.

The theater was full of people, enjoying the spectacle and laughing till they cried at the antics of the two Marionettes.

The play continued for a few minutes, and then suddenly, without any warning, Harlequin stopped talking. Turning toward the audience, he pointed to the rear of the orchestra, yelling wildly at the same time:

"Look, look! Am I asleep or awake? Or do I really see Pinocchio there?"

"Yes, yes! It is Pinocchio!" screamed Pulcinella.

"It is! It is!" shrieked Signora Rosaura, peeking in from the side of the stage.

"It is Pinocchio! It is Pinocchio!" yelled all the Marionettes, pouring out of the wings. "It is Pinocchio. It is our brother Pinocchio! Hurrah for Pinocchio!"

"Pinocchio, come up to me!" shouted Harlequin. "Come to the arms of your wooden brothers!"

At such a loving invitation, Pinocchio, with one leap from the back of the orchestra, found himself in the front rows. With another

leap, he was on the orchestra leader's head. With a third, he landed on the stage.

It is impossible to describe the shrieks of joy, the warm embraces, the knocks, and the friendly greetings with which that strange company of dramatic actors and actresses received Pinocchio.

It was a heart-rending spectacle, but the audience, seeing that the play had stopped, became angry and began to yell:

"The play, the play, we want the play!"

The yelling was of no use, for the Marionettes, instead of going on with their act, made twice as much racket as before, and, lifting up Pinocchio on their shoulders, carried him around the stage in triumph.

At that very moment, the Director came out of his room. He
had such a fearful appearance that one look at him would fill you
with horror. His beard was as black as pitch, and so long that it
reached from his chin down to his feet. His mouth was as wide
as an oven, his teeth like yellow fangs, and his eyes, two glowing

red coals. In his huge, hairy hands, a long whip, made of green snakes and black cats' tails twisted together, swished through the air in a dangerous way.

At the unexpected apparition, no one dared even to breathe. One could almost hear a fly go by. Those poor Marionettes, one and all, trembled like leaves in a storm.

"Why have you brought such excitement into my theater?" the huge fellow asked Pinocchio with the voice of an ogre suffering with a cold.

"Believe me, your Honor, the fault was not mine."

"Enough! Be quiet! I'll take care of you later."

As soon as the play was over, the Director went to the kitchen, where a fine big lamb was slowly turning on the spit. More

wood was needed to finish cooking it. He called Harlequin and Pulcinella and said to them:

"Bring that Marionette to me! He looks as if he were made of well-seasoned wood. He'll make a fine fire for this spit."

Harlequin and Pulcinella hesitated a bit. Then, frightened by a look from their master, they left the kitchen to obey him. A few minutes later they returned, carrying poor Pinocchio, who was wriggling and squirming like an eel and crying pitifully:

"Father, save me! I don't want to die! I don't want to die!"

CHAPTER 11

*Fire Eater sneezes
and forgives Pinoc-
chio, who saves his
friend, Harlequin,
from death.*

In the theater, great excitement reigned.

Fire Eater (this was really his name) was very ugly, but he was far from being as bad as he looked. Proof of this is that, when he saw the poor Marionette being brought in to him, struggling with fear and crying, "I don't want to die! I don't want to die!" he felt sorry for him and began first to waver and then to weaken. Finally, he could control himself no longer and gave a loud sneeze.

At that sneeze, Harlequin, who until then had been as sad as a weeping willow, smiled happily and leaning toward the Marionette, whispered to him:

"Good news, brother mine! Fire Eater has sneezed and this is a sign that he feels sorry for you. You are saved!"

For be it known that, while other people, when sad and sorrowful, weep and wipe their eyes, Fire Eater, on the other hand, had the strange habit of sneezing each time he felt unhappy. The way was just as good as any other to show the kindness of his heart.

After sneezing, Fire Eater, ugly as ever, cried to Pinocchio:

"Stop crying! Your wails give me a funny feeling down here in my stomach and—E—tchee!—E—tchee!" Two loud sneezes finished his speech.

"God bless you!" said Pinocchio.

"Thanks! Are your father and mother still living?" demanded Fire Eater.

"My father, yes. My mother I have never known."

"Your poor father would suffer terribly if I were to use you as firewood. Poor old man! I feel sorry for him! E—tchee! E—tchee! E—tchee!" Three more sneezes sounded, louder than ever.

"God bless you!" said Pinocchio.

"Thanks! However, I ought to

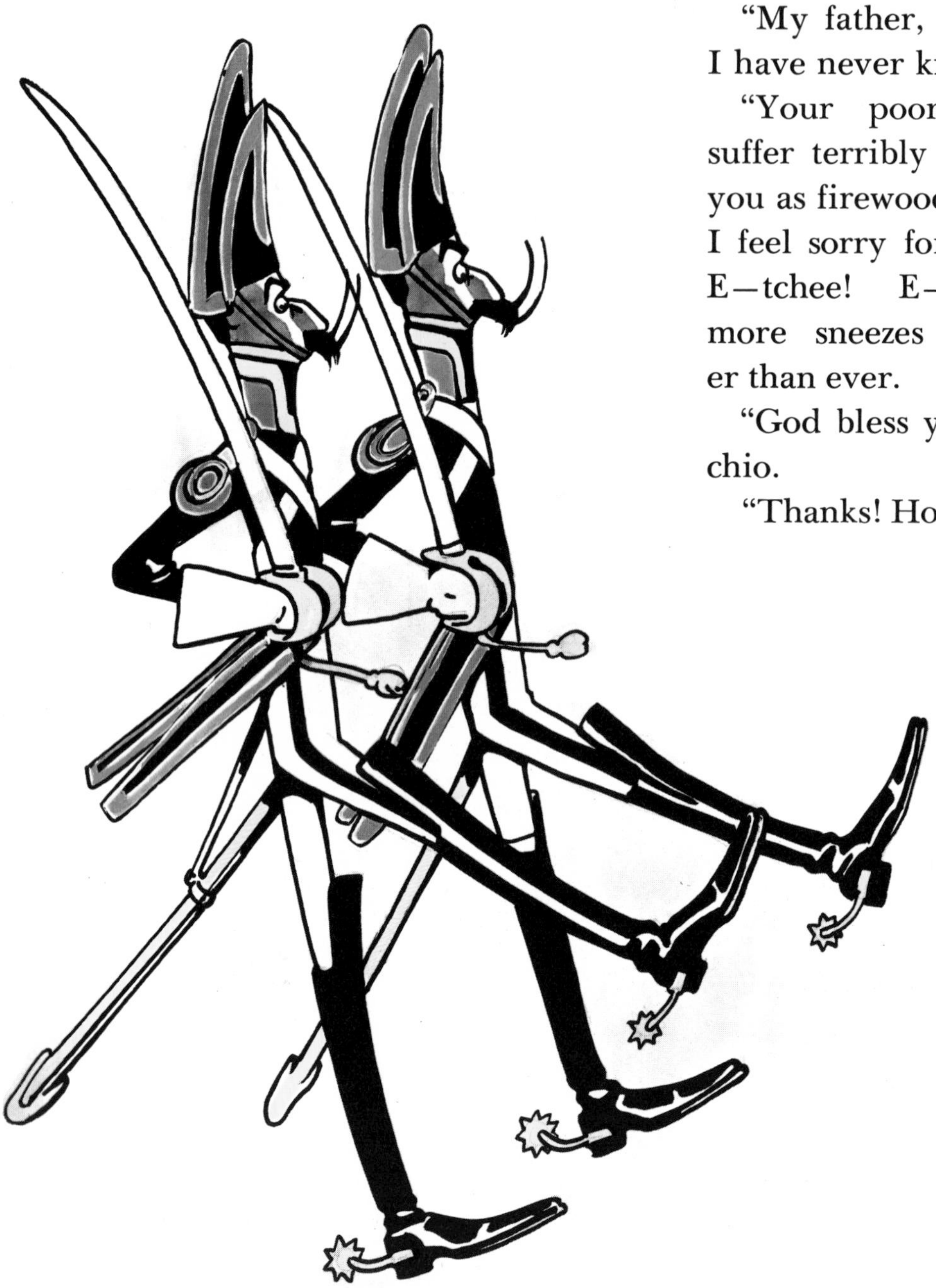

be sorry for myself, too, just now. My good dinner is spoiled. I have no more wood for the fire, and the lamb is only half cooked. Never mind! In your place I'll burn some other Marionette. Hey there! Officers!"

At the call, two wooden officers appeared, long and thin as a yard of rope, with queer hats on their heads and swords in their hands.

Fire Eater yelled at them in a hoarse voice:

"Take Harlequin, tie him, and throw him on the fire. I want my lamb well done!"

Think how poor Harlequin felt! He was so scared that his legs doubled up under him and he fell to the floor.

Pinocchio, at that heartbreaking sight, threw himself at the feet of Fire Eater and, weeping bitterly, asked in a pitiful voice which could scarcely be heard:

"Have pity, I beg of you, signore!"

"There are no signori here!"

"Have pity, kind sir!"

"There are no sirs here!"

"Have pity, your Excellency!"

On hearing himself addressed as your Excellency, the Director of the Marionette Theatre sat up very straight in his chair, stroked his long beard, and becoming suddenly kind and compassionate, smiled proudly as he said to Pinocchio:

"Well, what do you want from me now, Marionette?"

"I beg for mercy for my poor friend, Harlequin, who has never done the least harm in his life."

"There is no mercy here, Pinocchio. I have spared you. Harlequin must burn in your place. I am hungry and my dinner must be cooked."

"In that case," said Pinocchio proudly, as he stood up and flung away his cap of dough, "in that case, my duty is clear. Come, officers! Tie me up and throw me on those flames. No, it is not fair for poor Harlequin, the best friend that I have in the world, to die in my place!"

These brave words, said in a piercing voice, made all the other Marionettes cry. Even the officers, who were made of wood also, cried like two babies.

Fire Eater at first remained hard and cold as a piece of ice; but then, little by little, he softened and began to sneeze. And after four or five sneezes, he opened wide his arms and said to Pinocchio:

"You are a brave boy! Come to my arms and kiss me!"

Pinocchio ran to him and scurrying like a squirrel up the long black beard, he gave Fire Eater a loving kiss on the tip of his nose.

"Has pardon been granted to me?" asked poor Harlequin with a voice that was hardly a breath.

"Pardon is yours!" answered Fire Eater; and sighing and wagging his head, he added: "Well, tonight I shall have to eat my lamb only half cooked, but beware the next time, Marionettes."

At the news that pardon had been given, the Marionettes ran to the stage and, turning on all the lights, they danced and sang till dawn.

CHAPTER 12

*Fire Eater gives Pinocchio five
gold pieces for his father, Geppetto; but the Marionette meets a
Fox and a Cat and follows them.*

The next day Fire Eater called Pinocchio aside and asked him:

"What is your father's name?"

"Geppetto."

"And what is his trade?"

"He's a wood carver."

"Does he earn much?"

"He earns so much that he never has a penny in his pockets. Just think that, in order to buy me an A-B-C book for school, he had to sell the only coat he owned, a coat so full of darns and patches that it was a pity."

"Poor fellow! I feel sorry for him. Here, take these five gold pieces. Go, give them to him with my kindest regards."

Pinocchio, as may easily be imagined, thanked him a thousand

times. He kissed each Marionette in turn, even the officers, and, beside himself with joy, set out on his homeward journey.

He had gone barely half a mile when he met a lame Fox and a blind Cat, walking together like two good friends. The lame Fox leaned on the Cat, and the blind Cat let the Fox lead him along.

"Good morning, Pinocchio," said the Fox, greeting him courteously.

"How do you know my name?" asked the Marionette.

"I know your father well."

"Where have you seen him?"

"I saw him yesterday standing at the door of his house."

"And what was he doing?"

"He was in his shirt sleeves trembling with cold."

"Poor Father! But, after today, God willing, he will suffer no longer."

"Why?"

"Because I have become a rich man."

"You, a rich man?" said the Fox, and he began to laugh out

loud. The Cat was laughing also, but he tried to hide it by stroking his long whiskers.

"There is nothing to laugh at," cried Pinocchio angrily. "I am very sorry to make your mouth water, but these, as you know, are five new gold pieces."

And he pulled out the gold pieces which Fire Eater had given him.

At the cheerful tinkle of the gold, the Fox unconsciously held out his paw that was supposed to be lame, and the Cat opened wide his two eyes till they looked like live coals, but he closed them again so quickly that Pinocchio did not notice.

"And may I ask," inquired the Fox, "what you are going to do with all that money?"

"First of all," answered the Marionette, "I want to buy a fine new coat for my father, a coat of gold and silver with diamond buttons; after that, I'll buy an A-B-C book for myself."

"For yourself?"

"For myself. I want to go to school and study hard."

"Look at me," said the Fox. "For the silly reason of wanting to study, I have lost a paw."

"Look at me," said the Cat. "For the same foolish reason, I have lost the sight of both eyes."

At that moment, a Blackbird, perched on the fence along the road, called out sharp and clear:

"Pinocchio, do not listen to bad advice. If you do, you'll be sorry!"

Poor little Blackbird! If he had only kept his words to himself! In the twinkling of an eyelid, the Cat leaped on him, and ate him, feathers and all.

After eating the bird, he cleaned his whiskers, closed his eyes, and became blind once more.

"Poor Blackbird!" said Pinocchio to the Cat. "Why did you kill him?"

"I killed him to teach him a lesson. He talks too much. Next time he will keep his words to himself."

By this time the three companions had walked a long distance. Suddenly, the Fox stopped in his tracks and, turning to the Marionette, said to him:

"Do you want to double your gold pieces?"

"What do you mean?"

"Do you want one hundred, a thousand, two thousand gold pieces for your miserable five?"

"Yes, but how?"

"The way is very easy. Instead of returning home, come with us."

"And where will you take me?"

"To the City of Simple Simons."

Pinocchio thought a while and then said firmly:

"No, I don't want to go. Home is near, and I'm going where Father is waiting for me. How unhappy he must be that I have not yet returned! I have been a bad son, and the Talking Cricket was right when he said that a disobedient boy cannot be happy in this world. I have learned this at my own expense. Even last night in the theater, when Fire Eater…Brrrr!!!!!…The shivers run up and down my back at the mere thought of it."

"Well, then," said the Fox, "if you really want to go home, go ahead, but you'll be sorry."

"You'll be sorry," repeated the Cat.

"Think well, Pinocchio, you are turning your back on Dame Fortune."

"On Dame Fortune," repeated the Cat.

"Tomorrow your five gold pieces will be two thousand!"

"Two thousand!" repeated the Cat.

"But how can they possibly become so many?" asked Pinocchio wonderingly.

"I'll explain," said the Fox. "You must know that, just outside the City of Simple Simons, there is a blessed field called the Field of Wonders. In this field you dig a hole and in the hole you bury a gold piece. After covering up the hole with earth you water it well, sprinkle a bit of salt on it, and go to bed. During the night, the gold piece sprouts, grows, blossoms, and next morning you find a beautiful tree that is loaded with gold pieces."

"So that if I were to bury my five gold pieces," cried Pinocchio with growing wonder, "next morning I should find—how many?"

"It is very simple to figure out," answered the Fox. "Why, you can figure it on your fingers! Granted that each piece gives you five hundred, multiply five hundred by five. Next morning you will find twenty-five hundred new, sparkling gold pieces."

"Fine! Fine!" cried Pinocchio, dancing about with joy. "And as soon as I have them, I shall keep two thousand for myself and the other five hundred I'll give to you two."

"A gift for us?" cried the Fox, pretending to be insulted. "Why, of course not!"

"Of course not!" repeated the Cat.

"We do not work for gain," answered the Fox. "We work only to enrich others."

"To enrich others!" repeated the Cat.

"What good people," thought Pinocchio to himself. And forgetting his father, the new coat, the A-B-C book, and all his good resolutions, he said to the Fox and to the Cat:

"Let us go. I am with you."

CHAPTER 13

The Inn of the Red Lobster

Cat and Fox and Marionette walked and walked and walked. At last, toward evening, dead tired, they came to the Inn of the Red Lobster.

"Let us stop here a while," said the Fox, "to eat a bite and rest for a few hours. At midnight we'll start out again, for at dawn tomorrow we must be at the Field of Wonders."

They went into the Inn and all three sat down at the same table. However, not one of them was very hungry.

The poor Cat felt very weak, and he was able to eat only thirty-five mullets with tomato sauce and four portions of tripe with cheese. Moreover, as he was so in need of strength, he had to have four more helpings of butter and cheese.

The Fox, after a great deal of coaxing, tried his best to eat a little. The doctor had put him on a diet, and he had to be satisfied with a small hare dressed with a dozen young and tender spring chick-

ens. After the hare, he ordered some partridges, a few pheasants, a couple of rabbits, and a dozen frogs and lizards. That was all. He felt ill, he said, and could not eat another bite.

Pinocchio ate least of all. He asked for a bite of bread and a few nuts and then hardly touched them. The poor fellow, with his mind on the Field of Wonders, was suffering from a gold-piece indigestion.

Supper over, the Fox said to the Innkeeper:

"Give us two good rooms, one for Mr. Pinocchio and the other for me and my friend. Before starting out, we'll take a little nap. Remember to call us at midnight sharp, for we must continue on our journey."

"Yes sir," answered the Innkeeper, winking in a knowing way at the Fox and the Cat, as if to say, "I understand."

As soon as Pinocchio was in bed, he fell fast asleep and began to dream. He dreamed he was in the middle of a field. The field was full of vines heavy with grapes. The grapes were no other than gold coins which tinkled merrily as they swayed in the wind. They seemed to say, "Let him who wants us take us!"

Just as Pinocchio stretched out his hand to take a handful of them, he was awakened by three loud knocks at the door. It was the Innkeeper who had come to tell him that midnight had struck.

"Are my friends ready?" the Marionette asked him.

"Indeed, yes! They went two hours ago."

"Why in such a hurry?"

"Unfortunately the Cat received a telegram which said that his first-born was suffering from chilblains and was on the point of death. He could not even wait to say good-by to you."

"Did they pay for the supper?"

"How could they do such a thing? Being people of great refinement, they did not want to offend you so deeply as not to allow you the honor of paying the bill."

"Too bad! That offense would have been more than pleasing to me," said Pinocchio, scratching his head.

"Where did my good friends say they would wait for me?" he added.

"At the Field of Wonders, at sunrise tomorrow morning."

Pinocchio paid a gold piece for three suppers and started on his way toward the field that was to make him a rich man.

He walked on, not knowing where he was going, for it was dark, so dark that not a thing was visible. Round about him, not a leaf stirred. A few bats skimmed his nose now and again and scared him half to death. Once or twice he shouted, "Who goes there?" and the far-away hills echoed back to him, "Who goes there? Who goes there? Who goes . . .?"

As he walked, Pinocchio noticed a tiny insect glimmering on the trunk of a tree, a small being that glowed with a pale, soft light.

"Who are you?" he asked.

"I am the ghost of the Talking Cricket," answered the little being in a faint voice that sounded as if it came from a far-away world.

"What do you want?" asked the Marionette.

"I want to give you a few words of good advice. Return home and give the four gold pieces you have left to your poor old father who is weeping because he has not seen you for many a day."

"Tomorrow my father will be a rich man, for these four gold pieces will become two thousand."

"Don't listen to those who promise you wealth overnight, my boy. As a rule they are either fools or swindlers! Listen to me and go home."

"But I want to go on!"

"The hour is late!"

"I want to go on."

"The night is very dark."

"I want to go on."

"The road is dangerous."

"I want to go on."

"Remember that boys who insist on having their own way, sooner or later come to grief."

"The same nonsense. Good-by, Cricket."

"Good night, Pinocchio, and may Heaven preserve you from the Assassins."

There was silence for a minute and the light of the Talking Cricket disappeared suddenly, just as if someone had snuffed it out. Once again the road was plunged in darkness.

CHAPTER 14

Pinocchio, not having listened to the good advice of the Talking Cricket, falls into the hands of the Assassins.

"Dear, oh, dear! When I come to think of it," said the Marionette to himself, as he once more set out on his journey, "we boys are really very unlucky. Everybody scolds us, everybody gives us advice, everybody warns us. If we were to allow it, everyone would try to be father and mother to us; everyone, even the Talking Cricket. Take me, for example. Just because I would not listen to that bothersome Cricket, who knows how many misfortunes may be awaiting me! Assassins indeed! At least I have never believed in them, nor ever will. To speak sensibly, I think assassins have been invented by fathers and mothers to frighten children who want to run away at night. And then, even if I were to meet them on the road, what matter? I'll just run up to them, and say, 'Well, signori, what do you want? Remember that you can't fool with me! Run along and mind your business.' At such a speech, I can almost see those poor fellows running like the wind.

But in case they don't run away, I can always run myself . . ."

Pinocchio was not given time to argue any longer, for he thought he heard a slight rustle among the leaves behind him.

He turned to look and, behold, there in the darkness stood two big black shadows, wrapped from head to foot in black sacks. The two figures leaped toward him as softly as if they were ghosts.

"Here they come!" Pinocchio said to himself, and, not knowing where to hide the gold pieces, he stuck all four of them under his tongue.

He tried to run away, but hardly had he taken a step, when he felt his arms grasped and heard two horrible, deep voices say to him: "Your money or your life!"

On account of the gold pieces in his mouth, Pinocchio could not say a word, so he tried with head and hands and body to show, as best he could, that he was only a poor Marionette, without a penny in his pocket.

"Come, come, less nonsense, and out with your money," cried the two thieves in threatening voices.

Once more, Pinocchio's head and hands said, "I haven't a penny."

"Out with that money or you're a dead man," said the taller of the two Assassins.

"Dead man," repeated the other.

"And after having killed you, we will kill your father also."

"Your father also!"

"No, no, no, not my Father!" cried Pinocchio, wild with terror; but as he screamed, the gold pieces tinkled together in his mouth.

"Ah, you rascal! So that's the game! You have the money hidden under your tongue. Out with it!"

But Pinocchio was as stubborn as ever.

"Are you deaf? Wait, young man, we'll get it from you in a twinkling!"

One of them grabbed the Marionette by the nose and the other by the chin, and they pulled him unmercifully from side to side in order to make him open his mouth.

All was of no use. The Marionette's lips might have been nailed together. They would not open.

In desperation the smaller of the two Assassins pulled out a long knife from his pocket, and tried to pry Pinocchio's mouth open with it.

Quick as a flash, the Marionette sank his teeth deep into the Assassin's hand, bit it off and spat it out. Fancy his surprise when he saw that it was not a hand, but a cat's paw.

Encouraged by this first victory, he freed himself from the claws of his assailers and, leaping over the bushes along the road, ran swiftly across the fields. His pursuers were after him at once, like two dogs chasing a hare.

After running seven miles or so, Pinocchio was well-nigh exhausted. Seeing himself lost, he climbed up a giant pine tree and sat there to see what he could see. The Assassins tried to climb also, but they slipped and fell.

Far from giving up the chase, this only spurred them on. They gathered a bundle of wood, piled it up at the foot of the pine, and set fire to it. In a twinkling the tree began to sputter and burn like a candle blown by the wind. Pinocchio saw the flames climb higher and higher. Not wishing to end his days as a roasted Marionette, he jumped quickly to the

ground and off he went, the Assassins close to him, as before.

Dawn was breaking when, without any warning whatsoever, Pinocchio found his path barred by a deep pool full of water the color of muddy coffee.

What was there to do? With a "One, two, three!" he jumped clear across it. The Assassins jumped also, but not having measured their distance well—splash!!!—they fell right into the middle of the pool. Pinocchio, who heard the splash and felt it, too, cried out, laughing, but never stopping in his race:

"A pleasant bath to you, signori!"

He thought they must surely be drowned and turned his head to see. But there were the two somber figures still following him, though their black sacks were drenched and dripping with water.

CHAPTER 15

The Assassins chase Pinoc-chio, catch him, and hang him to the branch of a giant oak tree.

As he ran, the Marionette felt more and more certain that he would have to give himself up into the hands of his pursuers. Suddenly he saw a little cottage gleaming white as the snow among the trees of the forest.

"If I have enough breath left with which to reach that little house, I may be saved," he said to himself.

Not waiting another moment, he darted swiftly through the woods, the Assassins still after him.

After a hard race of almost an hour, tired and out of breath, Pinocchio finally reached the door of the cottage and knocked. No one answered.

He knocked again, harder than before, for behind him he heard the steps and the labored breathing of his persecutors. The same silence followed.

As knocking was of no use, Pinocchio, in despair, began to kick and bang against the door, as if he wanted to break it. At the noise, a window opened and a lovely maiden looked out. She had azure hair and a face white as wax. Her eyes were closed and her hands crossed on her breast. With a voice so weak that it hardly could be heard, she whispered:

"No one lives in this house. Everyone is dead."

"Won't you, at least, open the door for me?" cried Pinocchio in a beseeching voice.

"I also am dead."

"Dead? What are you doing at the window, then?"

"I am waiting for the coffin to take me away."

After these words, the little girl disappeared and the window closed without a sound.

"Oh, Lovely Maiden with Azure Hair," cried Pinocchio, "open, I beg of you. Take pity on a poor boy who is being chased by two Assass—"

He did not finish, for two powerful hands grasped him by the neck and the same two horrible voices growled threateningly: "Now we have you!"

The Marionette, seeing death dancing before him, trembled

so hard that the joints of his legs rattled and the coins tinkled under his tongue.

"Well," the Assassins asked, "will you open your mouth now or not? Ah! You do not answer? Very well, this time you shall open it."

Taking out two long, sharp knives, they struck two heavy blows on the Marionette's back.

Happily for him, Pinocchio was made of very hard wood and the knives broke into a thousand pieces. The Assassins looked at each other in dismay, holding the handles of the knives in their hands.

"I understand," said one of them to the other, "there is nothing left to do now but to hang him."

"To hang him," repeated the other.

They tied Pinocchio's hands behind his shoulders and slipped the noose around his neck. Throwing the rope over the high limb of a giant oak tree, they pulled till the poor Marionette hung far up in space.

Satisfied with their work, they sat on the grass waiting for Pinocchio to give his last gasp. But after three hours the Marionette's eyes were still open, his mouth still shut and his legs kicked harder than ever.

Tired of waiting, the Assassins called to him mockingly: "Good-by till tomorrow. When we return in the morning, we hope you'll be polite enough to let us find you dead and gone and with your mouth wide open." With these words they went.

A few minutes went by and then a wild wind started to blow. As it shrieked and moaned, the poor little sufferer was blown to and fro like the hammer of a bell. The rocking made him seasick and the noose, becoming tighter and tighter, choked him. Little by little a film covered his eyes.

Death was creeping nearer and nearer, and the Marionette still hoped for some good soul to come to his rescue, but no one

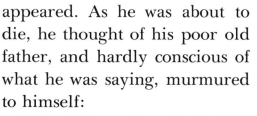

appeared. As he was about to die, he thought of his poor old father, and hardly conscious of what he was saying, murmured to himself:

"Oh, Father, dear Father! If you were only here!"

These were his last words. He closed his eyes, opened his mouth, stretched out his legs, and hung there, as if he were dead.

CHAPTER 16

The Lovely Maiden with Azure Hair sends for the poor Marionette, puts him to bed, and calls three Doctors to tell her if Pinocchio is dead or alive.

If the poor Marionette had dangled there much longer, all hope would have been lost. Luckily for him, the Lovely Maiden with Azure Hair once again looked out of her window. Filled with pity at the sight of the poor little fellow being knocked helplessly about by the wind, she clapped her hands sharply together three times.

At the signal, a loud whirr of wings in quick flight was heard and a large Falcon came and settled itself on the window ledge.

"What do you command, my charming Fairy?" asked the Falcon, bending his beak in deep reverence (for it must be known that, after all, the Lovely Maiden with Azure Hair was none other than a very kind Fairy who had lived, for more than a thousand years, in the vicinity of the forest).

"Do you see that Marionette hanging from the limb of that giant oak tree?"

"I see him."

"Very well. Fly immediately to him. With your strong beak, break the knot which holds him tied, take him down, and lay him softly on the grass at the foot of the oak."

The Falcon flew away and after two minutes returned, saying, "I have done what you have commanded."

"How did you find him? Alive or dead?"

"At first glance, I thought he was dead. But I found I was wrong, for as soon as I loosened the knot around his neck, he gave a long sigh and mumbled with a faint voice, 'Now I feel better!'"

The Fairy clapped her hands twice. A magnificent Poodle appeared, walking on his hind legs just like a man. He was dressed in court livery. A tricorn trimmed with gold lace was set at a rakish angle over a wig of white curls that dropped down to his waist. He wore a jaunty coat of chocolate-colored velvet, with diamond buttons, and with two huge pockets which were always filled with bones, dropped there at dinner by his loving mistress. Breeches of crimson velvet, silk stockings, and low, silver-buckled slippers completed his costume. His tail was encased in a blue silk covering, which was to protect it from the rain.

"Come, Medoro," said the Fairy to him. "Get my best coach ready and set out toward the forest. On reaching the oak tree, you will find a poor, half-dead Marionette stretched out on the grass. Lift him up tenderly, place him on the silken cushions of the coach, and bring him here to me."

The Poodle, to show that he understood, wagged his silk-covered tail two or three times and set off at a quick pace.

In a few minutes, a lovely little coach, made of glass, with lining as soft as whipped cream and chocolate pudding, and stuffed with canary feathers, pulled out of the stable. It was drawn by one hundred pairs of white mice, and the Poodle sat on the coachman's seat and snapped his whip gaily in the air, as if he were a real coachman in a hurry to get to his destination.

In a quarter of an hour the coach was back. The Fairy, who was

waiting at the door of the house, lifted the poor little Marionette in her arms, took him to a dainty room with mother-of-pearl walls, put him to bed, and sent immediately for the most famous doctors of the neighborhood to come to her.

One after another the doctors came, a Crow, an Owl, and a Talking Cricket.

"I should like to know, signori," said the Fairy, turning to the three doctors gathered about Pinocchio's bed, "I should like to know if this poor Marionette is dead or alive."

At this invitation, the Crow stepped out and felt Pinocchio's pulse, his nose, his little toe. Then he solemnly pronounced the following words:

"To my mind this Marionette is dead and gone; but if, by any evil chance, he were not, then that would be a sure sign that he is still alive!"

"I am sorry," said the Owl, "to have to contradict the Crow, my famous friend and colleague. To my mind this Marionette is alive; but if, by any evil chance, he were not, then that would be a sure sign that he is wholly dead!"

"And do you hold any opinion?" the Fairy asked the Talking Cricket.

"I say that a wise doctor, when he does not know what he is talking about, should know enough to keep his mouth shut. However, that Marionette is not a stranger to me. I have known him a long time!"

Pinocchio, who until then had been very quiet, shuddered so hard that the bed shook.

"That Marionette," continued the Talking Cricket, "is a rascal of the worst kind."

Pinocchio opened his eyes and closed them again.

"He is rude, lazy, a runaway."

Pinocchio hid his face under the sheets.

"That Marionette is a disobedient son who is breaking his father's heart!"

Long shuddering sobs were heard, cries, and deep sighs. Think how surprised everyone was when, on raising the sheets, they discovered Pinocchio half melted in tears!

"When the dead weep, they are beginning to recover," said the Crow solemnly.

"I am sorry to contradict my famous friend and colleague," said the Owl, "but as far as I'm concerned, I think that when the dead weep, it means they do not want to die."

CHAPTER 17

Pinocchio eats sugar, but refuses to take medicine. When the undertakers come for him, he drinks the medicine and feels better. Afterward he tells a lie and, in punishment, his nose grows longer and longer.

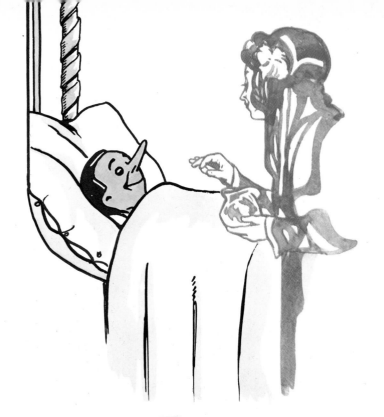

As soon as the three doctors had left the room, the Fairy went to Pinocchio's bed and, touching him on the forehead, noticed that he was burning with fever.

She took a glass of water, put a white powder into it, and, handing it to the Marionette, said lovingly to him:

"Drink this, and in a few days you'll be up and well."

Pinocchio looked at the glass, made a wry face, and asked in a whining voice: "Is it sweet or bitter?"

"It is bitter, but it is good for you."

"If it is bitter, I don't want it."

"Drink it!"

"I don't like anything bitter."

"Drink it and I'll give you a lump of sugar to take the bitter taste from your mouth."

"Where's the sugar?"

"Here it is," said the Fairy, taking a lump from a golden sugar bowl.

"I want the sugar first, then I'll drink the bitter water."

"Do you promise?"

"Yes."

The Fairy gave him the sugar and Pinocchio, after chewing and swallowing it in a twinkling, said, smacking his lips:

"If only sugar were medicine! I should take it every day."

"Now keep your promise and drink these few drops of water. They'll be good for you."

Pinocchio took the glass in both hands and stuck his nose into it. He lifted it to his mouth and once more stuck his nose into it.

"It is too bitter, much too bitter! I can't drink it."

"How do you know, when you haven't even tasted it?"

"I can imagine it. I smell it. I want another lump of sugar, then I'll drink it."

The Fairy, with all the patience of a good mother, gave him more sugar and again handed him the glass.

"I can't drink it like that," the Marionette said, making more wry faces.

"Why?"

"Because that feather pillow on my feet bothers me."

The Fairy took away the pillow.

"It's no use. I can't drink it even now."

"What's the matter now?"

"I don't like the way that door looks. It's half open."

The Fairy closed the door.

"I won't drink it," cried Pinocchio, bursting out crying. "I won't drink this awful water. I won't. I won't! No, no, no, no!"

"My boy, you'll be sorry."

"I don't care."

"You are very sick."

"I don't care."

"In a few hours the fever will take you far away to another world."

"I don't care."

"Aren't you afraid of death?"

"Not a bit. I'd rather die than drink that awful medicine."

At that moment, the door of the room flew open and in came four Rabbits as black as ink, carrying a small black coffin on their shoulders.

"What do you want from me?" asked Pinocchio.

"We have come for you," said the largest Rabbit.

"For me? But I'm not dead yet!"

"No, not dead yet; but you will be in a few moments since you have refused to take the medicine which would have made you well."

"Oh, Fairy, my Fairy," the Marionette cried out, "give me that glass! Quick, please! I don't want to die! No, no, not yet—not yet!"

And holding the glass with his two hands, he swallowed the medicine at one gulp.

"Well," said the four Rabbits, "this time we have made the trip for nothing."

And turning on their heels, they marched solemnly out of the room, carrying their little black coffin and muttering and grumbling between their teeth.

In a twinkling, Pinocchio felt fine. With one leap he was out of bed and into his clothes.

The Fairy, seeing him run and jump around the room gay as a bird on wing, said to him:

"My medicine was good for you, after all, wasn't it?"

"Good indeed! It has given me new life."

"Why, then, did I have to beg you so hard to make you drink it?"

"I'm a boy, you see, and all boys hate medicine more than they do sickness."

"What a shame! Boys ought to know, after all, that medicine, taken in time, can save them from much pain and even from death."

"Next time I won't have to be begged so hard. I'll remember those black Rabbits with

the black coffin on their shoulders and I'll take the glass and pouf!—down it will go!"

"Come here now and tell me how it came about that you found yourself in the hands of the Assassins."

"It happened that Fire Eater gave me five gold pieces to give to my Father, but on the way, I met a Fox and a Cat, who asked me, 'Do you want the five pieces to become two thousand?' And I said, 'Yes.' And they said, 'Come with us to the Field of Wonders.' And I said, 'Let's go.' Then they said, 'Let us stop at the Inn of the Red Lobster for dinner and after midnight we'll set out again.' We ate and went to sleep. When I awoke they were gone and I started out in the darkness all alone. On the road I met two Assassins dressed in black coal sacks, who said to me, 'Your money or your life!' and I said, 'I haven't any money'; for, you see, I had put the money under my tongue. One of them tried to put his hand in my mouth and I bit it off and spat it out; but it wasn't a hand, it was a cat's paw. And they ran after me and I ran and ran, till at last they caught me and tied my neck with a rope and hanged me to a tree, saying, 'Tomorrow we'll come back for you and you'll be dead and your mouth will be open, and then we'll take the gold pieces that you have hidden under your tongue.'"

"Where are the gold pieces now?" the Fairy asked.

"I lost them," answered Pinocchio, but he told a lie, for he had them in his pocket.

As he spoke, his nose, long though it was, became at least two inches longer.

"And where did you lose them?"

"In the wood near by."

At this second lie, his nose grew a few more inches.

"If you lost them in the near-by wood," said the Fairy, "we'll look for them and find them, for everything that is lost there is always found."

"Ah, now I remember," replied the Marionette, becoming more and more confused. "I did not lose the gold pieces, but I swallowed them when I drank the medicine."

At this third lie, his nose became longer than ever, so long that he could not even turn around. If he turned to the right, he knocked it against the bed or into the windowpanes; if he turned to the left, he struck the walls or the door; if he raised it a bit, he almost put the Fairy's eyes out.

The Fairy sat looking at him and laughing.

"Why do you laugh?" the Marionette asked her, worried now at the sight of his growing nose.

"I am laughing at your lies."

"How do you know I am lying?"

"Lies, my boy, are known in a moment. There are two kinds of lies, lies with short legs and lies with long noses. Yours, just now, happen to have long noses."

Pinocchio, not knowing where to hide his shame, tried to escape from the room, but his nose had become so long that he could not get it out of the door.

CHAPTER 18

*Pinocchio finds the Fox and the Cat again,
and goes with them to sow the gold pieces
in the Field of Wonders.*

Crying as if his heart would break, the Marionette mourned for hours over the length of his nose. No matter how he tried, it would not go through the door. The Fairy showed no pity toward him, as she was trying to teach him a good lesson, so that he would stop telling lies, the worst habit any boy may acquire. But when she saw him, pale with fright and with his eyes half out of his head from terror, she began to feel sorry for him and clapped her hands together. A thousand woodpeckers flew in through the window and settled themselves on Pinocchio's nose. They pecked and pecked so hard at that enormous nose that in a few moments, it was the same size as before.

"How good you are, my Fairy," said Pinocchio, drying his eyes, "and how much I love you!"

"I love you, too," answered the Fairy, "and if you wish to stay with me, you may be my little brother and I'll be your good little sister."

"I should like to stay—but what about my poor father?"

"I have thought of everything. Your father has been sent for and before night he will be here."

"Really?" cried Pinocchio joyfully. "Then, my good Fairy, if you are willing, I should like to go to meet him. I cannot wait to kiss that dear old man, who has suffered so much for my sake."

"Surely; go ahead, but be careful not to lose your way. Take the wood path and you'll surely meet him."

Pinocchio set out, and as soon as he found himself in the wood, he ran like a hare. When he reached the giant oak tree he stopped, for he thought he heard a rustle in the brush. He was right. There stood the Fox and the Cat, the two traveling companions with whom he had eaten at the Inn of the Red Lobster.

"Here comes our dear Pinocchio!" cried the Fox, hugging and kissing him. "How did you happen here?"

"How did you happen here?" repeated the Cat.

"It is a long story," said the Marionette. "Let me tell it to you. The other night, when you left me alone at the Inn, I met the Assassins on the road—"

"The Assassins? Oh, my poor friend! And what did they want?"

"They wanted my gold pieces."

"Rascals!" said the Fox.

"The worst sort of rascals!" added the Cat.

"But I began to run," continued the Marionette, "and they after me, until they overtook me and hanged me to the limb of that oak."

Pinocchio pointed to the giant oak near by.

"Could anything be worse?" said the Fox. "What an awful world to live in! Where shall we find a safe place for gentlemen like ourselves?"

As the Fox talked thus, Pinocchio noticed that the Cat carried his right paw in a sling.

"What happened to your paw?" he asked.

The Cat tried to answer, but he became so terribly twisted in his speech that the Fox had to help him out.

"My friend is too modest to answer. I'll answer for him. About an hour ago, we met an old wolf on the road. He was half starved and begged for help. Having nothing to give him, what do you think my friend did out of the kindness of his heart? With his teeth, he bit off the paw of his front foot and threw it at that poor beast, so that he might have something to eat."

As he spoke, the Fox wiped off a tear.

Pinocchio, almost in tears himself, whispered in the Cat's ear:

"If all the cats were like you, how lucky the mice would be!"

"And what are you doing here?" the Fox asked the Marionette.

"I am waiting for my father, who will be here at any moment now."

"And your gold pieces?"

"I still have them in my pocket, except one which I spent at the Inn of the Red Lobster."

"To think that those four gold pieces might become two thousand tomorrow. Why don't you listen to me? Why don't you sow them in the Field of Wonders?"

"Today it is impossible. I'll go with you some other time."

"Another day will be too late," said the Fox.

"Why?"

"Because that field has been bought by a very rich man, and today is the last day that it will be open to the public."

"How far is this Field of Wonders?"

"Only two miles away. Will you come with us? We'll be there in half an hour. You can sow the money, and, after a few minutes, you will gather your two thousand coins and return home rich. Are you coming?"

Pinocchio hesitated a moment before answering, for he remembered the good Fairy, Old Geppetto, and the advice of the Talking Cricket. Then he ended by doing what all boys do, when they have no heart and little brain. He shrugged his shoulders and said to the Fox and the Cat:

"Let us go! I am with you."

And they went.

They walked and walked for half a day at least and at last they

came to the town called the City of Simple Simons. As soon as they entered the town, Pinocchio noticed that all the streets were filled with hairless dogs, yawning from hunger; with sheared sheep, trembling with cold; with combless chickens, begging for a grain of wheat; with large butterflies, unable to use their wings because they had sold all their lovely colors; with tailless peacocks, ashamed to show themselves; and with bedraggled pheasants, scuttling away hurriedly, grieving for their bright feathers of gold and silver, lost to them forever.

Through this crowd of paupers and beggars, a beautiful coach passed now and again. Within it sat either a Fox, a Hawk, or a Vulture.

"Where is the Field of Wonders?" asked Pinocchio, growing tired of waiting.

"Be patient. It is only a few more steps away."

They passed through the city and, just outside the walls, they stepped into a lonely field, which looked more or less like any other field.

"Here we are," said the Fox to the Marionette. "Dig a hole here and put the gold pieces into it."

The Marionette obeyed. He dug the hole, put the four gold pieces into it, and covered them up very carefully.

"Now," said the Fox, "go to that near-by brook, bring back a pail full of water, and sprinkle it over the spot."

Pinocchio followed the directions closely, but, as he had no pail, he pulled off his shoe, filled it with water, and sprinkled the earth which covered the gold. Then he asked:

"Anything else?"

"Nothing else," answered the Fox. "Now we can go. Return here within twenty minutes and you will find the vine grown and the branches filled with gold pieces."

Pinocchio, beside himself with joy, thanked the Fox and the Cat many times and promised them each a beautiful gift.

"We don't want any of your gifts," answered the two rogues. "It is enough for us that we have helped you to become rich with little or no trouble. For this we are as happy as kings."

They said good-by to Pinocchio and, wishing him good luck, went on their way.

CHAPTER 19

*Pinocchio is robbed
of his gold pieces
and, in punish-
ment, is sentenced
to four months
in prison.*

If the Marionette had been told to wait a day instead of twenty minutes, the time could not have seemed longer to him. He walked impatiently to and fro and finally turned his nose toward the Field of Wonders.

And as he walked with hurried steps, his heart beat with an excited tic, tac, tic, tac, just as if it were a wall clock, and his busy brain kept thinking:

"What if, instead of a thousand, I should find two thousand? Or if, instead of two thousand, I should find five thousand—or one hundred thousand? I'll build myself a beautiful palace, with a thousand stables filled with a thousand wooden horses to play with, a cellar overflowing with lemonade and ice cream soda, and a library of candies and fruits, cakes and cookies."

Thus amusing himself with fancies, he came to the field. There he stopped to see if, by any chance, a vine filled with gold coins was in sight. But he saw nothing! He took a few steps forward, and still nothing! He stepped into the field. He went up to the place where he had dug the hole and buried the gold pieces. Again nothing! Pinocchio became very thoughtful and, forgetting his good manners altogether, he pulled a hand out of his pocket and gave his head a thorough scratching.

As he did so, he heard a hearty burst of laughter close to his head. He turned sharply, and there, just above him on the branch of a tree, sat a large Parrot, busily preening his feathers.

"What are you laughing at?" Pinocchio asked peevishly.

"I am laughing because, in preening my feathers, I tickled myself under the wings."

The Marionette did not answer. He walked to the brook, filled his shoe with water, and once more sprinkled the ground which covered the gold pieces.

140

Another burst of laughter, even more impertinent than the first, was heard in the quiet field.

"Well," cried the Marionette, angrily this time, "may I know, Mr. Parrot, what amuses you so?"

"I am laughing at those simpletons who believe everything they hear and who allow themselves to be caught so easily in the traps set for them."

"Do you, perhaps, mean me?"

"I certainly do mean you, poor Pinocchio—you who are such a little silly as to believe that gold can be sown in a field just like beans or squash. I, too, believed that once and today I am very sorry for it. Today (but too late!) I have reached the conclusion that, in order to come by money honestly, one must work and know how to earn it with hand or brain."

"I don't know what you are talking about," said the Marionette, who was beginning to tremble with fear.

"Too bad! I'll explain myself better," said the Parrot. "While you were away in the city the Fox and the Cat returned here in a great hurry. They took the four gold pieces which you have buried and ran away as fast as the wind. If you can catch them, you're a brave one!"

Pinocchio's mouth opened wide. He would not believe the Parrot's words and began to dig away furiously at the earth. He dug and he dug till the hole was as big as himself, but no money was there. Every penny was gone.

In desperation, he ran to the city and went straight to the courthouse to report the robbery to the magistrate.

The judge was a Monkey, a large Gorilla venerable with age. A flowing white beard covered his chest and he wore gold-rimmed spectacles from which the glasses had dropped out. The reason for wearing these, he said, was that his eyes had been weakened by the work of many years.

Pinocchio, standing before him, told his pitiful tale, word by word. He gave the names and the descriptions of the robbers and begged for justice.

The Judge listened to him with great patience. A kind look shone in his eyes. He became very much interested in the story; he felt moved; he almost wept. When the Marionette had no more to say, the Judge put out his hand and rang a bell.

At the sound, two large Mastiffs appeared, dressed in Carabineers' uniforms.

Then the magistrate, pointing to Pinocchio, said in a very solemn voice:

"This poor simpleton has been robbed of four gold pieces. Take him, therefore, and throw him into prison."

The Marionette, on hearing this sentence passed upon him, was thoroughly stunned. He tried to protest, but the two officers clapped their paws on his mouth and hustled him away to jail.

There he had to remain for four long, weary months. And if it had not been for a very lucky chance, he probably would have had to stay there longer. For, my dear children, you must know that it happened just then that the young emperor who ruled over the City of Simple Simons had gained a great victory over his enemy, and in celebration thereof, he had ordered illumi-

nations, fireworks, shows of all kinds, and, best of all, the opening of all prison doors.

"If the others go, I go, too," said Pinocchio to the Jailer.

"Not you," answered the Jailer. "You are one of those—"

"I beg your pardon," interrupted Pinocchio, "I, too, am a thief."

"In that case you also are free," said the Jailer. Taking off his cap, he bowed low and opened the door of the prison, and Pinocchio ran out and away, with never a look backward.

CHAPTER 20

*Freed from prison, Pinoc-
chio sets out to return to
the Fairy; but on the way
he meets a Serpent and
later is caught in a trap.*

Fancy the happiness of Pinocchio on finding himself free! Without saying yes or no, he fled from the city and set out on the road that was to take him back to the house of the lovely Fairy.

It had rained for many days, and the road was so muddy that, at times, Pinocchio sank down almost to his knees.

But he kept on bravely.

Tormented by the wish to see his father and his fairy sister with azure hair, he raced like a greyhound. As he ran, he was splashed with mud even up to his cap.

"How unhappy I have been," he said to himself. "And yet I deserve everything, for I am certainly very stubborn and stupid! I will always have my own way. I won't listen to those who love

me and who have more brains than I. But from now on, I'll be different and I'll try to become a most obedient boy. I have found out, beyond any doubt whatever, that disobedient boys are certainly far from happy, and that, in the long run, they always lose out. I wonder if Father is waiting for me. Will I find him at the Fairy's house? It is so long, poor man, since I have seen him, and I do so want his love and his kisses. And will the Fairy ever forgive me for all I have done? She who has been so good to me and to whom I owe my life! Can there be a worse or more heartless boy than I am anywhere?"

As he spoke, he stopped suddenly, frozen with terror.

What was the matter? An immense Serpent lay stretched across the road—a Serpent with a bright green skin, fiery eyes which glowed and burned, and a pointed tail that smoked like a chimney.

How frightened was poor Pinocchio! He ran back wildly for half a mile, and at last settled himself atop a heap of stones to wait for the Serpent to go on his way and leave the road clear for him.

He waited an hour; two hours; three hours; but the Serpent was always there, and even from afar one could see the flash of

his red eyes and the column of smoke which rose from his long, pointed tail.

Pinocchio, trying to feel very brave, walked straight up to him and said in a sweet, soothing voice:

"I beg your pardon, Mr. Serpent, would you be so kind as to step aside to let me pass?"

He might as well have talked to a wall. The Serpent never moved.

Once more, in the same sweet voice, he spoke:

"You must know, Mr Serpent, that I am going home where my father is waiting for me. It is so long since I have seen him! Would you mind very much if I passed?"

He waited for some sign of an answer to his questions, but the answer did not come. On the contrary, the green Serpent, who had seemed, until then, wide awake and full of life, became suddenly very quiet and still. His eyes closed and his tail stopped smoking.

"Is he dead, I wonder?" said Pinocchio, rubbing his hands together happily. Without a moment's hesitation, he started to step over him, but he had just raised one leg when the Serpent shot up like a spring and the Marionette fell head over heels backward. He fell so awkwardly that his head stuck in the mud, and there he stood with his legs straight up in the air.

At the sight of the Marionette kicking and squirming like a young whirlwind, the Serpent laughed so heartily and so long that at last he burst an artery and died on the spot.

Pinocchio freed himself from his awkward position and once more began to run in order to reach the Fairy's house before dark. As he went, the pangs of hunger grew so strong that, unable to withstand them, he jumped into a field to pick a few grapes that tempted him. Woe to him!

No sooner had he reached the grapevine than—crack! went his legs.

The poor Marionette was caught in a trap set there by a Farmer for some Weasels which came every night to steal his chickens.

CHAPTER 21

Pinocchio is caught by a Farmer, who uses him as a watchdog for his chicken coop.

Pinocchio, as you may well imagine, began to scream and weep and beg; but all was of no use, for no houses were to be seen and not a soul passed by on the road.

Night came on.

A little because of the sharp pain in his legs, a little because of fright at finding himself alone in the darkness of the field, the Marionette was about to faint, when he saw a tiny Glowworm flickering by. He called to her and said:

"Dear little Glowworm, will you set me free?"

"Poor little fellow!" replied the Glowworm, stopping to look at him with pity. "How came you to be caught in this trap?"

"I stepped into this lonely field to take a few grapes and—"

"Are the grapes yours?"

"No."

"Who has taught you to take things that do not belong to you?"

"I was hungry."

"Hunger, my boy, is no reason for taking something which belongs to another."

"It's true, it's true!" cried Pinocchio in tears. "I won't do it again."

Just then, the conversation was interrupted by approaching footsteps. It was the owner of the field, who was coming on tiptoes to see if, by chance, he had caught the Weasels which had been eating his chickens.

Great was his surprise when, on holding up his lantern, he saw that, instead of a Weasel, he had caught a boy!

"Ah, you little thief!" said the Farmer in an angry voice. "So you are the one who steals my chickens!"

"Not I! No, no!" cried Pinocchio, sobbing bitterly. "I came here only to take a very few grapes."

"He who steals grapes may very easily steal chickens also.

156

Take my word for it, I'll give you a lesson that you'll remember for a long while."

He opened the trap, grabbed the Marionette by the collar, and carried him to the house as if he were a puppy.

When he reached the yard in front of the house, he flung him to the ground, put a foot on his neck, and said to him roughly: "It is late now and it's time for bed. Tomorrow we'll settle matters. In the meantime, since my watchdog died today, you may take his place and guard my henhouse."

No sooner said than done. He slipped a dog collar around Pinocchio's neck and tightened it so that it would not come off. A long iron chain was tied to the collar. The other end of the chain was nailed to the wall.

"If tonight it should happen to rain," said the Farmer, "you can sleep in that little doghouse near-by, where you will find plenty of straw for a soft bed. It has been Melampo's bed for three years, and it will be good enough for you. And if, by any chance, any thieves should come, be sure to bark!"

After this last warning, the

Farmer went into the house and closed the door and barred it.

Poor Pinocchio huddled close to the doghouse more dead than alive from cold, hunger, and fright. Now and again he pulled and tugged at the collar which nearly choked him and cried out in a weak voice:

"I deserve it! Yes, I deserve it! I have been nothing but a truant and a vagabond. I have never obeyed anyone and I have always done as I pleased. If I were only like so many others and had studied and worked and stayed with my poor old father, I should not find myself here now, in this field and in the darkness, taking the place of a farmer's watchdog. Oh, if I could start all over again! But what is done can't be undone, and I must be patient!"

After this little sermon to himself, which came from the very depths of his heart, Pinocchio went into the doghouse and fell asleep.

CHAPTER 22

*Pinocchio discovers the
thieves and, as a re-
ward for faithfulness,
he regains his liberty.*

Even though a boy may be very unhappy, he very seldom loses sleep over his worries. The Marionette, being no exception to this rule, slept on peacefully for a few hours till well along toward midnight, when he was awakened by strange whisperings and stealthy sounds coming from the yard. He stuck his nose out of the doghouse and saw four slender, hairy animals. They were Weasels, small animals very fond of both eggs and chickens. One of them left her companions and, going to the door of the doghouse, said in a sweet voice:

"Good evening, Melampo."

"My name is not Melampo," answered Pinocchio.

"Who are you, then?"

"I am Pinocchio."

"What are you doing here?"

"I'm the watchdog."

"But where is Melampo? Where is the old dog who used to live in this house?"

"He died this morning."

"Died? Poor beast! He was so good! Still, judging by your face, I think you, too, are a good-natured dog."

"I beg your pardon, I am not a dog."

"What are you, then?"

"I am a Marionette."

"Are you taking the place of the watchdog?"

"I'm sorry to say that I am. I'm being punished."

"Well, I shall make the same terms with you that we had with the dead Melampo. I am sure you will be glad to hear them."

"And what are the terms?"

"This is our plan: We'll come once in a while, as in the past, to pay a visit to this henhouse, and we'll take away eight chickens. Of these, seven are for us, and one for you, provided, of course, that you will make believe you are sleeping and will not bark for the Farmer."

"Did Melampo really do that?" asked Pinocchio.

"Indeed he did, and because of that we were the best of friends. Sleep away peacefully, and remember that before we go we shall leave you a nice fat chicken all ready for your breakfast in the morning. Is that understood?"

"Even too well," answered Pinocchio. And shaking his head in a threatening manner, he seemed to say, "We'll talk this over in a few minutes, my friends."

As soon as the four Weasels had talked things over, they

went straight to the chicken
coop which stood close to the
doghouse. Digging busily with
both feet and claws, they opened
the little door and slipped in.
But they were no sooner in
than they heard the door close
with a sharp bang.

The one who had done the
trick was Pinocchio, who, not
satisfied with that, dragged
a heavy stone in front of it. That
done, he started to bark. And
he barked as if he were a real
watchdog: "Bow, wow, wow!
Bow, wow!"

The Farmer heard the loud
barks and jumped out of bed. Taking his gun, he leaped to the window and shouted: "What's the matter?"

"The thieves are here," answered Pinocchio.

"Where are they?"

"In the chicken coop."

"I'll come down in a second."

And, in fact, he was down in the yard in a twinkling and running toward the chicken coop.

He opened the door, pulled out the Weasels one by one, and, after tying them in a bag, said to them in a happy voice: "You're in my hands at last! I could punish you now, but I'll wait! In the morning you may come with me to the inn and there you'll make a fine dinner for some hungry mortal. It is really too great an honor for you, one you do not deserve; but, as you see, I am really a very kind and generous man and I am going to do this for you!"

Then he went up to Pinocchio and began to pet and caress him.

"How did you ever find them out so quickly? And to think that Melampo, my faithful Melampo, never saw them in all these years!"

The Marionette could have told, then and there, all he knew about the shameful contract between the dog and the Weasels, but thinking of the dead dog, he said to himself: "Melampo is dead. What is the use of accusing him? The dead are gone and they cannot defend themselves. The best thing to do is to leave them in peace!"

"Were you awake or asleep when they came?" continued the Farmer.

"I was asleep," answered Pinocchio, "but they awakened me with their whisperings. One of them even came to the door of the doghouse and said to me, 'If you promise not to bark, we will make you a present of one of the chickens for your breakfast.' Did you hear that? They had the audacity to make such a proposition as that to me! For you must know that, though I am a very wicked Marionette full of faults, still I never have been, nor ever shall be, bribed."

"Fine boy!" cried the Farmer, slapping him on the shoulder in a friendly way. "You ought to be proud of yourself. And to show you what I think of you, you are free from this instant!"

And he slipped the dog collar from his neck.

CHAPTER 23

*Pinocchio weeps upon
learning that the Lovely
Maiden with Azure Hair
is dead. He meets a Pigeon,
who carries him to
the seashore. He throws
himself into the sea to go
to the aid of his father.*

As soon as Pinocchio no longer felt the shameful weight of the dog collar around his neck, he started to run across the fields and meadows, and never stopped till he came to the main road that was to take him to the Fairy's house.

When he reached it, he looked into the valley far below him and there he saw the wood where unluckily he had met the Fox and the Cat, and the tall oak tree where he had been hanged; but though he searched far and near, he could not see the house where the Fairy with the Azure Hair lived.

He became terribly frightened and, running as fast as he could, he finally came to the spot where it had once stood. The little house was no longer there. In its place lay a small marble slab, which bore this sad inscription:

HERE LIES

THE LOVELY FAIRY WITH AZURE HAIR

WHO DIED OF GRIEF

WHEN ABANDONED BY

HER LITTLE BROTHER PINOCCHIO

The poor Marionette was heartbroken at reading these words. He fell to the ground and, covering the cold marble with kisses, burst into bitter tears. He cried all night, and dawn found him still there, though his tears had dried and only hard, dry sobs shook his wooden frame. But these were so loud that they could be heard by the faraway hills.

As he sobbed he said to himself:

"Oh, my Fairy, my dear, dear Fairy, why did you die? Why did I not die, who am so bad, instead of you, who are so good? And my father—where can he be? Please, dear Fairy, tell me where

he is and I shall never, never leave him again! You are not really dead, are you? If you love me, you will come back, alive as before. Don't you feel sorry for me? I'm so lonely. If the two Assassins come, they'll hang me again from the giant oak tree and I will really die, this time. What shall I do alone in the world? Now that you are dead and my father is lost, where shall I eat? Where shall I sleep? Who will make my new clothes? Oh, I want to die! Yes, I want to die! Oh, oh, oh!"

Poor Pinocchio! He even tried to tear his hair, but as it was only painted on his wooden head, he could not even pull it.

Just then a large Pigeon flew far above him. Seeing the Marionette, he cried to him:

"Tell me, little boy, what are you doing there?"

169

"Can't you see? I'm crying," cried Pinocchio, lifting his head toward the voice and rubbing his eyes with his sleeve.

"Tell me," asked the Pigeon, "do you by chance know of a Marionette, Pinocchio by name?"

"Pinocchio! Did you say Pinocchio?" replied the Marionette, jumping to his feet. "Why, I am Pinocchio!"

At this answer, the Pigeon flew swiftly down to the earth. He was much larger than a turkey.

"Then you know Geppetto also?"

"Do I know him? He's my father, my poor, dear father! Has he, perhaps, spoken to you of me? Will you take me to him? Is he still alive? Answer me, please! Is he still alive?"

"I left him three days ago on the shore of a large sea."

"What was he doing?"

"He was building a little boat with which to cross the ocean. For the last four months, that poor man has been wandering around Europe, looking for you. Not having found you yet, he has made up his mind to look for you in the New World, far across the ocean."

"How far is it from here to the shore?" asked Pinocchio anxiously.

"More than fifty miles."

"Fifty miles? Oh, dear Pigeon, how I wish I had your wings!"

"If you want to come, I'll take you with me."

"How?"

"Astride my back. Are you very heavy?"

"Heavy? Not at all. I'm only a feather."

"Very well."

Saying nothing more, Pinocchio jumped on the Pigeon's back and, as he settled himself, he cried out gaily:

"Gallop on, gallop on, my pretty steed! I'm in a great hurry."

The Pigeon flew away, and in a few minutes he had reached the clouds. The Marionette looked to see what was below them. His head swam and he was so frightened that he clutched wildly at the Pigeon's neck to keep himself from falling.

They flew all day. Toward evening the Pigeon said:

"I'm very thirsty!"

"And I'm very hungry!" said Pinocchio.

"Let us stop a few minutes at that pigeon coop down there. Then we can go on and be at the seashore in the morning."

They went into the empty coop and there they found nothing but a bowl of water and a small basket filled with chickpeas.

The Marionette had always hated chickpeas. According to him, they had always made him sick; but that night he ate them with a relish. As he finished them, he turned to the Pigeon and said:

"I never should have thought that chickpeas could be so good!"

"You must remember, my boy," answered the Pigeon, "that hunger is the best sauce!"

After resting a few minutes longer, they set out again. The next morning they were at the seashore.

Pinocchio jumped off the Pigeon's back, and the Pigeon, not wanting any thanks for a kind deed, flew away swiftly and disappeared.

The shore was full of people, shrieking and tearing their hair as they looked toward the sea.

"What has happened?" asked Pinocchio of a little old woman.

"A poor old father lost his only son some time ago and today he built a tiny boat for himself in order to go in search of him across the ocean. The water is very rough and we're afraid he will be drowned."

"Where is the little boat?"

"There. Straight down there," answered the little old woman, pointing to a tiny shadow, no bigger than a nutshell, floating on the sea.

Pinocchio looked closely for a few minutes and then gave a sharp cry:

"It's my father! It's my father!"

Meanwhile, the little boat, tossed about by the angry waters, appeared and disappeared in the waves. And Pinocchio, standing on a high rock, tired out with searching, waved to him with hand and cap and even with his nose.

It looked as if Geppetto, though far away from the shore, recognized his son, for he took off his cap and waved also. He seemed to be trying to make everyone understand that he would come back if he were able, but the sea was so heavy that he could do

nothing with his oars. Suddenly a huge wave came and the boat disappeared.

They waited and waited for it, but it was gone.

"Poor man!" said the fisher folk on the shore, whispering a prayer as they turned to go home.

Just then a desperate cry was heard. Turning around, the fisher folk saw Pinocchio dive into the sea and heard him cry out:

"I'll save him! I'll save my father!"

The Marionette, being made of wood, floated easily along and swam like a fish in the rough water. Now and again he disappeared only to reappear once more. In a twinkling, he was far away from land. At last he was completely lost to view.

"Poor boy!" cried the fisher folk on the shore, and again they mumbled a few prayers as they returned home.

174

CHAPTER 24

Pinocchio reaches the Island of the Busy Bees and finds the Fairy once more.

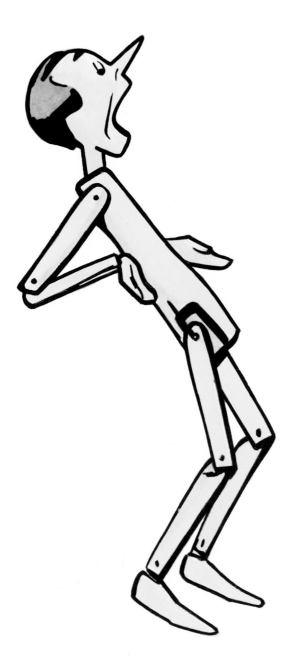

Pinocchio, spurred on by the hope of finding his father and of being in time to save him, swam all night long.

And what a horrible night it was! It poured rain, it hailed, it thundered, and the lightning was so bright that it turned the night into day.

At dawn, he saw, not far away from him, a long stretch of sand. It was an island in the middle of the sea.

Pinocchio tried his best to get there, but he couldn't. The waves played with him and tossed him about as if he were a twig or a bit of straw. At last, and luckily for him, a tremendous wave tossed him to the very spot where he wanted to be. The blow from the wave was so strong that, as he fell to the ground, his joints cracked and almost broke. But, nothing daunted, he jumped to his feet and cried:

"Once more I have escaped with my life!"

Little by little the sky cleared. The sun came out in full splendor and the sea became as calm as a lake.

Then the Marionette took off his clothes and laid them on the sand to dry. He looked over the waters to see whether he might catch sight of a boat with a little man in it. He searched and he searched, but he saw nothing except sea and sky and far away a few sails, so small that they might have been birds.

"If only I knew the name of this island!" he said to himself. "If I even knew what kind of people I would find here! But whom shall I ask? There is no one here."

The idea of finding himself in so lonesome a spot made him so sad that he was about to cry, but just then he saw a big Fish swimming near-by, with his head far out of the water.

Not knowing what to call him, the Marionette said to him:

"Hey there, Mr. Fish, may I have a word with you?"

"Even two, if you want," answered the fish, who happened to be a very polite Dolphin.

"Will you please tell me if, on this island, there are places where one may eat without necessarily being eaten?"

"Surely, there are," answered the Dolphin. "In fact you'll find one not far from this spot."

"And how shall I get there?"

"Take that path on your left and follow your nose. You can't go wrong."

"Tell me another thing. You who travel day and night through the sea, did you not perhaps meet a little boat with my father in it?"

"And who is your father?"

"He is the best father in the world, even as I am the worst son that can be found."

"In the storm of last night," answered the Dolphin, "the little boat must have been swamped."

"And my father?"

"By this time, he must have been swallowed by the Terrible Shark, which, for the last few

days, has been bringing terror to these waters."

"Is this Shark very big?" asked Pinocchio, who was beginning to tremble with fright.

"Is he big?" replied the Dolphin. "Just to give you an idea of his size, let me tell you that he is larger than a five-story building and that he has a mouth so big and so deep, that a whole train and engine could easily get into it."

"Mother mine!" cried the Marionette, scared to death; and dressing himself as fast as he could, he turned to the Dolphin and said:

"Farewell, Mr. Fish. Pardon the bother, and many thanks for your kindness."

This said, he took the path at so swift a gait that he seemed to fly, and at every small sound he heard, he turned in fear to see whether the Terrible Shark, five stories high and with a train in his mouth, was following him.

After walking a half hour, he came to a small country called the Land of the Busy Bees. The streets were filled with people running to and fro about their tasks. Everyone worked, everyone had something to do. Even if one were to search with a lantern, not one idle man or one

tramp could have been found.

"I understand," said Pinocchio at once wearily, "this is no place for me! I was not born for work."

But in the meantime, he began to feel hungry, for it was twenty-four hours since he had eaten.

What was to be done?

There were only two means left to him in order to get a bite to eat. He had either to work or to beg.

He was ashamed to beg, because his father had always preached to him that begging should be done only by the sick or the old. He had said that the real poor in this world, deserving of our pity and help, were only those who, either through age or sickness, had lost the means of earning their bread with their own hands. All others should work, and if they didn't, and went hungry, so much the worse for them.

Just then a man passed by, worn out and wet with perspiration, pulling, with difficulty, two heavy carts filled with coal.

Pinocchio looked at him and, judging him by his looks to be a kind man, said to him with eyes downcast in shame:

"Will you be so good as to give me a penny, for I am faint with hunger?"

"Not only one penny," answered the Coal Man. "I'll give you four if you will help me pull these two wagons."

"I am surprised!" answered the Marionette, very much offended. "I wish you to know that I never have been a donkey, nor have I ever pulled a wagon."

"So much the better for you!" answered the Coal Man. "Then, my boy, if you are really faint with hunger, eat two slices of your pride; and I hope they don't give you indigestion."

A few minutes after, a Bricklayer passed by, carrying a pail full of plaster on his shoulder.

"Good man, will you be kind enough to give a penny to a poor boy who is yawning from hunger?"

"Gladly," answered the Bricklayer. "Come with me and carry some plaster, and instead of one penny, I'll give you five."

"But the plaster is heavy," answered Pinocchio, "and the work too hard for me."

"If the work is too hard for you, my boy, enjoy your yawns and may they bring you luck!"

In less than a half hour, at least twenty people passed and Pinocchio begged of each one, but they all answered:

"Aren't you ashamed? Instead of being a beggar in the streets, why don't you look for work and earn your own bread?"

Finally a little woman went by carrying two water jugs.

"Good woman, will you allow

me to have a drink from one of your jugs?" asked Pinocchio, who was burning up with thirst.

"With pleasure, my boy!" she answered, setting the two jugs on the ground before him.

When Pinocchio had had his fill, he grumbled, as he wiped his mouth:

"My thirst is gone. If I could only as easily get rid of my hunger!"

On hearing these words, the good little woman immediately said:

"If you help me to carry these jugs home, I'll give you a slice of bread."

Pinocchio looked at the jug and said neither yes nor no.

"And with the bread, I'll give you a nice dish of cauliflower with white sauce on it."

Pinocchio gave the jug another look and said neither yes nor no.

"And after the cauliflower, some cake and jam."

At this last bribery, Pinocchio could no longer resist and said firmly:

"Very well. I'll take the jug home for you."

The jug was very heavy, and the Marionette, not being strong enough to carry it with his hands, had to put it on his head.

When they arrived home, the little woman made Pinocchio sit down at a small table and placed before him the bread, the cauliflower, and the cake. Pinocchio did not eat; he devoured. His stomach seemed a bottomless pit.

His hunger finally appeased, he raised his head to thank his kind benefactress. But he had not looked at her long when he gave a cry of surprise and sat there with his eyes wide open, his fork in the air, and his mouth filled with bread and cauliflower.

"Why all this surprise?" asked the good woman, laughing.

"Because—" answered Pinocchio, stammering and stuttering, "because—you look like—you remind me of—yes, yes, the same voice, the same eyes, the same hair—yes, yes, yes, you also have the same azure hair she had—Oh, my little Fairy, my little Fairy! Tell me that it is you! Don't make me cry any longer! If you only knew! I have cried so much, I have suffered so!"

And Pinocchio threw himself on the floor and clasped the knees of the mysterious little woman.

CHAPTER 25

Pinocchio promises the Fairy to be good and to study, as he is growing tired of being a Marionette, and wishes to become a real boy.

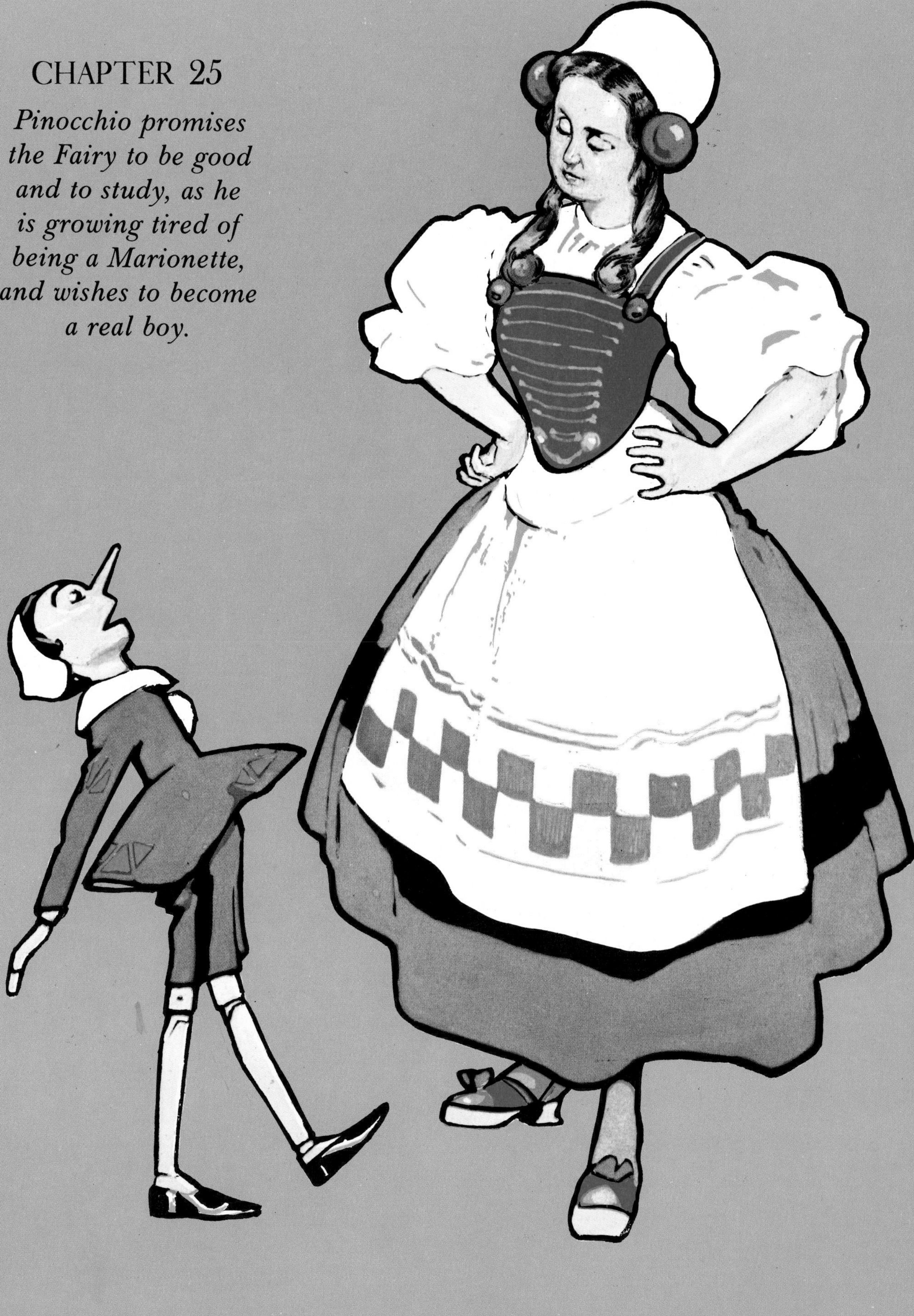

If Pinocchio cried much longer, the little woman thought he would melt away, so she finally admitted that she was the little Fairy with Azure Hair.

"You rascal of a Marionette! How did you know it was I?" she asked, laughing.

"My love for you told me who you were."

"Do you remember? You left me when I was a little girl and now you find me a grown woman. I am so old, I could almost be your mother!"

"I am very glad of that, for then I can call you mother instead of sister. For a long time I have wanted a mother, just like other boys. But how did you grow so quickly?"

"That's a secret!"

"Tell it to me. I also want to grow a little. Look at me! I have never grown higher than a penny's worth of cheese."

"But you can't grow," answered the Fairy.

"Why not?"

"Because Marionettes never grow. They are born Marionettes, they live Marionettes, and they die Marionettes."

"Oh, I'm tired of always being a Marionette!" cried Pinocchio disgustedly. "It's about time for me to grow into a man as everyone else does."

"And you will if you deserve it—"

"Really? What can I do to deserve it?"

"It's a very simple matter. Try to act like a well-behaved child."

"Don't you think I do?"

"Far from it! Good boys are obedient, and you, on the contrary—"

"And I never obey."

"Good boys love study and work, but you—"

"And I, on the contrary, am a lazy fellow and a tramp all year round."

"Good boys always tell the truth."

"And I always tell lies."

"Good boys go gladly to school."

"And I get sick if I go to school. From now on I'll be different."

"Do you promise?"

"I promise. I want to become a good boy and be a comfort to my father. Where is my poor father now?"

"I do not know."

"Will I ever be lucky enough to find him and embrace him once more?"

"I think so. Indeed, I am sure of it."

At this answer, Pinocchio's happiness was very great. He grasped the Fairy's hands and kissed them so hard that it looked as if he had lost his head. Then lifting his face, he looked at her lovingly and asked: "Tell me, little Mother, it isn't true that you are dead, is it?"

"It doesn't seem so," answered the Fairy, smiling.

"If you only knew how I suffered and how I wept when I read 'Here lies—'"

"I know it, and for that I have forgiven you. The depth of your sorrow made me see that you have a kind heart. There is always hope for boys with hearts such as yours, though they may often be very mischievous. This is the reason why I have come so far to look for you. From now on, I'll be your own little mother."

"Oh! How lovely!" cried Pinocchio, jumping with joy.

"You will obey me always and do as I wish?"

"Gladly, very gladly, more than gladly!"

"Beginning tomorrow," said the Fairy, "you'll go to school every day."

Pinocchio's face fell a little.

"Then you will choose the trade you like best."

Pinocchio became more serious.

"What are you mumbling to yourself?" asked the Fairy.

"I was just saying," whined the Marionette in a whisper, "that it seems too late for me to go to school now."

"No, indeed. Remember it is never too late to learn."

"But I don't want either trade or profession."

"Why?"

"Because work wearies me!"

"My dear boy," said the Fairy, "people who speak as you do usually end their days either in a prison or in a hospital. A man, remember, whether rich or poor, should do something in this world. No one can find happiness without work. Woe betide the lazy fellow! Laziness is a serious illness and one must cure it immediately; yes, even from early childhood. If not, it will kill you in the end."

These words touched Pinocchio's heart. He lifted his eyes to his Fairy and said seriously:

"I'll work; I'll study; I'll do all you tell me. After all, the life of a Marionette has grown very tiresome to me and I want to become a boy, no matter how hard it is. You promise that, do you not?"

"Yes, I promise, and now it is up to you."

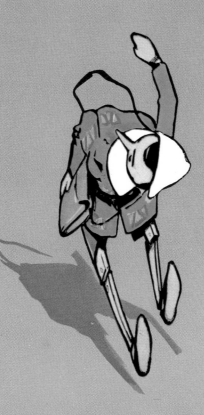

CHAPTER 26

*Pinocchio goes to the sea-
shore with his friends to
see the Terrible Shark.*

In the morning, bright and early, Pinocchio started for school.

Imagine what the boys said when they saw a Marionette enter the classroom! They laughed until they cried. Everyone played tricks on him. One pulled his hat off, another tugged at his coat, a third tried to paint a mustache under his nose. One even attempted to tie strings to his feet and his hands to make him dance.

For a while Pinocchio was very calm and quiet. Finally, however, he lost all patience and turning to his tormentors, he said to them threateningly:

"Careful, boys, I haven't come here to be made fun of. I'll respect you and I want you to respect me."

"Hurrah for Dr. Know-all! You have spoken like a printed book!" howled the boys, bursting with laughter. One of them, more impudent than the rest, put out his hand to pull the Marionette's nose.

But he was not quick enough, for Pinocchio stretched his leg under the table and kicked him hard on the shin.

"Oh, what hard feet!" cried the boy, rubbing the spot where the Marionette had kicked him.

"And what elbows! They are even harder than the feet!" shouted another one, who, because of some other trick, had received a blow in the stomach.

With that kick and that blow Pinocchio gained everybody's favor. Everyone admired him, danced attendance upon him, petted and caressed him.

As the days passed into weeks, even the teacher praised him, for he saw him attentive, hard working, and wide awake, always the first to come in the morning, and the last to leave when school was over.

Pinocchio's only fault was that he had too many friends. Among these were many well-known rascals, who cared not a jot for study or for success.

The teacher warned him each day, and even the good Fairy repeated to him many times:

"Take care, Pinocchio! Those bad companions will sooner or later make you lose your love for study. Some day they will lead you astray."

"There's no such danger," answered the Marionette, shrugging his shoulders and pointing to his forehead as if to say, "I'm too wise."

So it happened that one day, as he was walking to school, he met some boys who ran up to him and said:

"Have you heard the news?"

"No!"

"A Shark as big as a mountain has been seen near the shore."

"Really? I wonder if it could be the same one I heard of when my father was drowned?"

"We are going to see it. Are you coming?"

"No, not I. I must go to school."

"What do you care about school? You can go there tomorrow. With a lesson more or less, we are always the same donkeys."

"And what will the teacher say?"

"Let him talk. He is paid to grumble all day long."

"And my mother?"

"Mothers don't know anything," answered those scamps.

"Do you know what I'll do?" said Pinocchio. "For certain reasons of mine, I, too, want to see that Shark; but I'll go after school. I can see him then as well as now."

"Poor simpleton!" cried one of the boys. "Do you think that a fish of that size will stand there waiting for you? He turns and off he goes, and no one will ever be the wiser."

"How long does it take from here to the shore?" asked the Marionette.

"One hour there and back."

"Very well, then. Let's see who gets there first!" cried Pinocchio.

At the signal, the little troop, with books under their arms, dashed across the fields. Pinocchio led the way, running as if on wings, the others following as fast as they could.

Now and again, he looked back and, seeing his followers hot and tired, and with tongues hanging out, he laughed out heartily. Unhappy boy! If he had only known then the dreadful things that were to happen to him on account of his disobedience!

CHAPTER 27

The great battle between Pinocchio and his play-mates. One is wounded. Pinocchio is arrested.

Going like the wind, Pinocchio took but a very short time to reach the shore. He glanced all about him, but there was no sign of a Shark. The sea was as smooth as glass.

"Hey there, boys! Where's that Shark?" he asked, turning to his playmates.

"He may have gone for his breakfast," said one of them, laughing.

"Or, perhaps, he went to bed for a little nap," said another, laughing also.

From the answers and the laughter which followed them, Pinocchio understood that the boys had played a trick on him.

"What now?" he said angrily to them. "What's the joke?"

"Oh, the joke's on you!" cried his tormentors, laughing more heartily than ever, and dancing gaily around the Marionette.

"And that is—?"

"That we have made you stay out of school to come with us. Aren't you ashamed of being such a goody-goody, and of studying so hard? You never have a bit of enjoyment."

"And what is it to you, if I do study?"

"What does the teacher think of us, you mean?"

"Why?"

"Don't you see? If you study and we don't, we pay for it. After all, it's only fair to look out for ourselves."

"What do you want me to do?"

"Hate school and books and teachers, as we all do. They are your worst enemies, you know, and they like to make you as unhappy as they can."

"And if I go on studying, what will you do to me?"

"You'll pay for it!"

"Really, you amuse me," answered the Marionette, nodding his head.

"Hey, Pinocchio," cried the tallest of them all, "that will do. We are tired of hearing you bragging about yourself, you little turkey cock! You may not be afraid of us, but remember we are not afraid of you, either! You are alone, you know, and we are seven."

"Like the seven sins," said Pinocchio, still laughing.

"Did you hear that? He has insulted us all. He has called us sins."

"Pinocchio, apologize for that, or look out!"

"Cuck—oo!" said the Marionette, mocking them with his thumb to his nose.

"You'll be sorry!"

"Cuck—oo!"

"We'll whip you soundly!"

"Cuck—oo!"

"You'll go home with a broken nose!"

"Cuck—oo!"

"Very well, then! Take that, and keep it for your supper," called out the boldest of his tormentors.

And with the words, he gave Pinocchio a terrible blow on the head.

Pinocchio answered with another blow, and that was the signal for the beginning of the fray. In a few moments, the fight raged hot and heavy on both sides.

Pinocchio, although alone, defended himself bravely. With those two wooden feet of his, he worked so fast that his opponents kept at a respectful distance. Wherever they landed, they left their painful mark and the boys could only run away and howl.

Enraged at not being able to fight the Marionette at close quar-

ters, they started to throw all kinds of books at him. Readers, ge-
ographies, histories, grammars flew in all directions. But Pinocchio was keen of eye and swift of movement, and the books
only passed over his head, landed in the sea, and disappeared.

The fish, thinking they might be good to eat, came to the top
of the water in great numbers. Some took a nibble, some took a
bite, but no sooner had they tasted a page or two, than they spat
them out with a wry face, as if to say:

"What a horrid taste! Our own food is so much better!"

Meanwhile, the battle waxed more and more furious. At the
noise, a large Crab crawled slowly out of the water and, with a
voice that sounded like a trombone suffering from a cold, he
cried out:

"Stop fighting, you rascals! These battles between boys rarely
end well. Trouble is sure to come to you!"

Poor Crab! He might as well have spoken to the wind. Instead of listening to his good advice, Pinocchio turned to him and said as roughly as he knew how:

"Keep quiet, ugly Crab! It would be better for you to chew a few cough drops to get rid of that cold you have. Go to bed and sleep! You will feel better in the morning."

In the meantime, the boys, having used all their books, looked around for new ammunition. Seeing Pinocchio's bundle lying idle near-by, they somehow managed to get hold of it.

One of the books was a very large volume, an arithmetic text, heavily bound in leather. It was Pinocchio's pride. Among all his books, he liked that one the best.

Thinking it would make a fine missile, one of the boys took hold of it and threw it with all his strength at Pinocchio's head. But instead of hitting the Marionette, the book struck one of the other boys, who, as pale as a ghost, cried out faintly, "Oh, Mother, help! I'm dying!" and fell senseless to the ground.

At the sight of that pale little corpse, the boys were so frightened that they turned tail and ran. In a few moments, all had disappeared.

All except Pinocchio. Although scared to death by the horror of what had been done, he ran to the sea and soaked his handkerchief in the cool water and with it bathed the head of his poor little schoolmate. Sobbing bitterly, he called to him, saying:

"Eugene! My poor Eugene! Open your eyes and look at me! Why don't you answer? I was not the one who hit you, you know. Believe me, I didn't do it. Open your eyes, Eugene? If you keep them shut, I'll die, too. Oh, dear me, how shall I ever go home now? How shall I ever look at my little mother again? What will happen to me? Where shall I go? Where shall I hide? Oh, how much better it would have been, a thousand times better, if only I had gone to school! Why did I listen to those boys? They always were a bad influence! And to think that the teacher had told me— and my mother, too!—'Beware of bad company!' That's what she said. But I'm stubborn and proud. I listen, but always I do as I wish. And then I pay. I've never had a moment's peace since I've been born! Oh, dear! What will become of me? What will become of me?"

Pinocchio went on crying and moaning and beating his head. Again and again he called to his little friend, when suddenly he heard heavy steps approaching.

He looked up and saw two tall Carabineers near him.

"What are you doing stretched out on the ground?" they asked Pinocchio.

"I'm helping this schoolfellow of mine."

"Has he fainted?"

"I should say so," said one of the Carabineers, bending to look at Eugene. "This boy has been wounded on the temple. Who has hurt him?"

"Not I," stammered the Marionette, who had hardly a breath left in his whole body.

"If it wasn't you, who was it, then?"

"Not I," repeated Pinocchio.

"And with what was he wounded?"

"With this book," and the Marionette picked up the arithmetic text to show it to the officer.

"And whose book is this?"

"Mine."

"Enough. Not another word! Get up as quickly as you can and come along with us."

"But I—"

"Come with us!"

"But I am innocent."

"Come with us!"

Before starting out, the officers called out to several fishermen passing by in a boat and said to them:

"Take care of this little fellow who has been hurt. Take him home and bind his wounds. Tomorrow we'll come after him."

They then took hold of Pinocchio and, putting him between

them, said to him in a rough voice: "March! And go quickly, or it will be the worse for you!"

They did not have to repeat their words. The Marionette walked swiftly along the road to the village. But the poor fellow hardly knew what he was about. He thought he was in a nightmare. He felt ill. His eyes saw everything double, his legs trembled, his tongue was dry, and, try as he might, he could not utter a single word. Yet, in spite of this numbness of feeling, he suffered keenly at the thought of passing under the windows of his good little Fairy's house. What would she say on seeing him between two Carabineers?

They had just reached the village, when a sudden gust of wind blew off Pinocchio's cap and made it go sailing far down the street.

"Would you allow me," the Marionette asked the Carabineers, "to run after my cap?"

"Very well, go; but hurry."

The Marionette went, picked up his cap—but instead of putting it on his head, he stuck it between his teeth and then raced toward the sea.

He went like a bullet out of a gun.

The Carabineers, judging that it would be very difficult to catch him, sent a large Mastiff after him, one that had won first prize in all the dog races. Pinocchio ran fast and the Dog ran faster. At so much noise, the people hung out of the windows or gathered in the street, anxious to see the end of the contest. But they were disappointed, for the Dog and Pinocchio raised so much dust on the road that, after a few moments, it was impossible to see them.

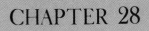

CHAPTER 28

*Pinocchio runs the
danger of being fried
in a pan like a fish.*

During that wild chase, Pinocchio lived through a terrible moment when he almost gave himself up as lost. This was when Alidoro (that was the Mastiff's name), in a frenzy of running, came so near that he was on the very point of reaching him.

The Marionette heard, close behind him, the labored breathing of the beast who was fast on his trail, and now and again even felt his hot breath blow over him.

Luckily, by this time, he was very near the shore, and the sea was in sight; in fact, only a few short steps away.

As soon as he set foot on the beach, Pinocchio gave a leap and fell into the water. Alidoro tried to stop, but as he was running very fast, he couldn't, and he, too, landed far out in the sea. Strange though it may seem, the Dog could not swim. He beat the water with his paws to hold himself up, but the harder he tried, the deeper

he sank. As he stuck his head out once more, the poor fellow's eyes were bulging and he barked out wildly, "I drown! I drown!"

"Drown!" answered Pinocchio from afar, happy at his escape.

"Help, Pinocchio, dear little Pinocchio! Save me from death!"

At those cries of suffering, the Marionette, who after all had a very kind heart, was moved to compassion. He turned toward the poor animal and said to him:

"But if I help you, will you promise not to bother me again by running after me?"

"I promise! I promise! Only hurry, for if you wait another second, I'll be dead and gone!"

Pinocchio hesitated still another minute. Then, remembering how his father had often told him that a kind deed is never lost,

he swam to Alidoro and, catching hold of his tail, dragged him to the shore.

The poor Dog was so weak he could not stand. He had swallowed so much salt water that he was swollen like a balloon. However, Pinocchio, not wishing to trust him too much, threw himself once again into the sea. As he swam away, he called out:

216

"Good-by, Alidoro, good luck and remember me to the family!"

"Good-by, little Pinocchio," answered the Dog. "A thousand thanks for having saved me from death. You did me a good turn, and, in this world, what is given is always returned. If the chance comes, I shall be there."

Pinocchio went on swimming close to shore. At last he thought he had reached a safe place. Glancing up and down the beach, he saw the opening of a cave out of which rose a spiral of smoke.

"In that cave," he said to himself, "there must be a fire. So much the better. I'll dry my clothes and warm myself, and then—well—"

His mind made up, Pinocchio swam to the rocks, but as he started to climb, he felt something under him lifting him up higher and higher. He tried to escape, but he was too late. To his great surprise, he found himself in a huge net, amid a crowd of fish of all kinds and sizes, who were fighting and struggling desperately to free themselves.

At the same time, he saw a Fisherman come out of the cave, a Fisherman so ugly that Pinocchio thought he was a sea monster. In place of hair, his head was covered by a thick bush of green grass. Green was the skin of his body, green were his eyes, green was the long, long beard that reached down to his feet. He looked like a giant lizard with legs and arms.

When the Fisherman pulled the net out of the sea, he cried out joyfully:

"Blessed Providence! Once more I'll have a fine meal of fish."

"Thank Heaven, I'm not a fish!" said Pinocchio to himself, trying with these words to find a little courage.

The Fisherman took the net and the fish to the cave, a dark, gloomy, smoky place. In the middle of it, a pan full of oil sizzled over a smoky fire, sending out a repelling odor of tallow that took away one's breath.

"Now, let's see what kind of fish we have caught today," said the Green Fisherman. He put a hand as big as a spade into the net and pulled out a handful of mullets.

"Fine mullets, these!" he said, after looking at them and smelling them with pleasure. After that, he threw them into a large, empty tub.

Many times he repeated this performance. As he pulled each fish out of the net, his mouth watered with the thought of the good dinner coming, and he said:

"Fine fish, these bass!"

"Very tasty, these whitefish!"

"Delicious flounders, these!"

"What splendid crabs!"

"And these dear little anchovies, with their heads still on!"

As you can well imagine, the bass, the flounders, the whitefish, and even the little anchovies all went together into the tub to keep the mullets company. The last to come out of the net was Pinocchio.

As soon as the Fisherman pulled him out, his green eyes opened wide with surprise, and he cried out in fear:

"What kind of fish is this? I don't remember ever eating anything like it."

He looked at him closely and after turning him over and over, he said at last:

"I understand. He must be a crab!"

Pinocchio, mortified at being taken for a crab, said resentfully:

"What nonsense! A crab indeed! I am no such thing. Beware how you deal with me! I am a Marionette, I want you to know."

"A Marionette?" asked the Fisherman. "I must admit that a Marionette fish is, for me, an entirely new kind of fish. So much the better. I'll eat you with greater relish."

"Eat me? But can't you understand that I'm not a fish? Can't you hear that I speak and think as you do?"

"It's true," answered the Fisherman; "but since I see that you are a fish, well able to talk and think as I do, I'll treat you with all due respect."

"And that is—"

"That, as a sign of my particular esteem, I'll leave to you the choice of the manner in which you are to be cooked. Do you wish to be fried in a pan, or do you prefer to be cooked with tomato sauce?"

"To tell you the truth," answered Pinocchio, "if I must choose, I should much rather go free so I may return home!"

"Are you fooling? Do you think that I want to lose the opportunity to taste such a rare fish? A Marionette fish does not come very often to these seas. Leave it to me. I'll fry you in the pan with the others. I know you'll like it. It's always a comfort to find oneself in good company."

The unlucky Marionette, hearing this, began to cry and wail and beg. With tears streaming down his cheeks, he said:

"How much better it would have been for me to go to school! I did listen to my playmates and now I am paying for it! Oh! Oh! Oh!"

And as he struggled and squirmed like an eel to escape from him, the Green Fisherman took a stout cord and tied him hand and foot, and threw him into the bottom of the tub with the others.

Then he pulled a wooden bowl full of flour out of a cupboard and started to roll the fish into it, one by one. When they were white with it, he threw them into the pan. The first to dance in the hot oil were the mullets, the bass followed, then the whitefish, the flounders, and the anchovies. Pinocchio's turn came last. Seeing himself so near to death (and such a horrible death!) he began to tremble so with fright that he had no voice left with which to beg for his life.

The poor boy beseeched only with his eyes. But the Green Fisherman, not even noticing that it was he, turned him over and over in the flour until he looked like a Marionette made of chalk.

Then he took him by the head and—

CHAPTER 29

Pinocchio returns to the Fairy's house and she promises him that, on the morrow, he will cease to be a Marionette and become a boy. A wonderful party of coffee-and-milk to celebrate the great event.

Mindful of what the Fisherman had said, Pinocchio knew that all hope of being saved had gone. He closed his eyes and waited for the final moment.

Suddenly, a large Dog, attracted by the odor of the boiling oil, came running into the cave.

"Get out!" cried the Fisherman threateningly and still holding onto the Marionette, who was all covered with flour.

But the poor Dog was very hungry, and whining and wagging his tail, he tried to say:

"Give me a bite of the fish and I'll go in peace."

"Get out, I say!" repeated the Fisherman.

And he drew back his foot to give the Dog a kick.

Then the Dog, who, being really hungry, would take no refusal, turned in a rage toward the Fisherman and bared his terrible fangs. And at that moment, a pitiful little voice was heard saying: "Save me, Alidoro; if you don't, I fry!"

The Dog immediately recognized Pinocchio's voice. Great

was his surprise to find that the voice came from the little flour-covered bundle that the Fisherman held in his hand.

Then what did he do? With one great leap, he grasped that bundle in his mouth and, holding it lightly between his teeth, ran through the door and disappeared like a flash!

The Fisherman, angry at see-

ing his meal snatched from under his nose, ran after the Dog, but a bad fit of coughing made him stop and turn back.

Meanwhile, Alidoro, as soon as he had found the road which led to the village, stopped and dropped Pinocchio softly to the ground.

"How much I do thank you!" said the Marionette.

"It is not necessary," answered the Dog. "You saved me once, and what is given is always returned. We are in this world to help one another."

"But how did you get in that cave?"

"I was lying here on the sand more dead than alive, when an appetizing odor of fried fish came to me. That odor tickled my hunger and I followed it. Oh, if I had come a moment later!"

"Don't speak about it," wailed Pinocchio, still trembling with

225

fright. "Don't say a word. If you had come a moment later, I would be fried, eaten, and digested by this time. Brrrrrr! I shiver at the mere thought of it."

Alidoro laughingly held out his paw to the Marionette, who shook it heartily, feeling that now he and the Dog were good friends. Then they bid each other good-by and the Dog went home.

Pinocchio, left alone, walked toward a little hut near by, where an old man sat at the door sunning himself, and asked:

"Tell me, good man, have you heard anything of a poor boy with a wounded head, whose name was Eugene?"

"The boy was brought to this hut and now—"

"Now he is dead?" Pinocchio interrupted sorrowfully.

"No, he is now alive and he has already returned home."

"Really? Really?" cried the Marionette, jumping around with joy. "Then the wound was not serious?"

"But it might have been—and even mortal," answered the old man, "for a heavy book was thrown at his head."

"And who threw it?"

"A schoolmate of his, a certain Pinocchio."

"And who is this Pinocchio?" asked the Marionette, feigning ignorance.

"They say he is a mischief-maker, a tramp, a street urchin—"

"Calumnies! All calumnies!"

"Do you know this Pinocchio?"

"By sight!" answered the Marionette.

"And what do you think of him?" asked the old man.

"I think he's a very good boy, fond of study, obedient, kind to his father, and to his whole family—"

As he was telling all these enormous lies about himself, Pinocchio touched his nose and found it twice as long as it should be. Scared out of his wits, he cried out:

"Don't listen to me, good man! All the wonderful things I have said are not true at all. I know Pinocchio well and he is indeed a very wicked fellow, lazy and disobedient, who instead of going to school, runs away with his playmates to have a good time."

At this speech, his nose returned to its natural size.

"Why are you so pale?" the old man asked suddenly.

"Let me tell you. Without knowing it, I rubbed myself against a newly painted wall," he lied, ashamed to say that he had been made ready for the frying pan.

"What have you done with your coat and your hat and your breeches?"

"I met thieves and they robbed me. Tell me, my good man, have you not, perhaps, a little suit to give me, so that I may go home?"

"My boy, as for clothes, I have only a bag in which I keep hops. If you want it, take it. There it is."

Pinocchio did not wait for him to repeat his words. He took the bag, which happened to be empty, and after cutting a big hole at the top and two at the sides, he slipped into it as if it

were a shirt. Lightly clad as he was, he started out toward the village.

Along the way he felt very uneasy. In fact he was so unhappy that he went along taking two steps forward and one back, and as he went he said to himself:

"How shall I ever face my good little Fairy? What will she say when she sees me? Will she forgive this last trick of mine? I am sure she won't. Oh, no, she won't. And I deserve it, as usual! For I am a rascal, fine on promises which I never keep!"

He came to the village late at night. It was so dark he could see nothing and it was raining pitchforks.

Pinocchio went straight to the Fairy's house, firmly resolved to knock at the door.

When he found himself there, he lost courage and ran back a few steps. A second time he came to the door and again he ran back. A third time he repeated his performance. The fourth time, before he had time to lose his courage, he grasped the knocker and made a faint sound with it.

He waited and waited and waited. Finally, after a full half hour, a top-floor window (the house had four stories) opened and Pinocchio saw a large Snail look out. A tiny light glowed on top of her head.

"Who knocks at this late hour?" she called.

228

"Is the Fairy home?" asked the Marionette.

"The Fairy is asleep and does not wish to be disturbed. Who are you?"

"It is I."

"Who's I?"

"Pinocchio."

"Who is Pinocchio?"

"The Marionette; the one who lives in the Fairy's house."

"Oh, I understand," said the Snail. "Wait for me there. I'll come down to open the door for you."

"Hurry, I beg of you, for I am dying of cold."

"My boy, I am a snail and snails are never in a hurry."

An hour passed, two hours; and the door was still closed. Pinocchio, who was trembling with fear and shivering from the cold rain on his back, knocked a second time, this time louder than before.

At that second knock, a window on the third floor opened and the same Snail looked out.

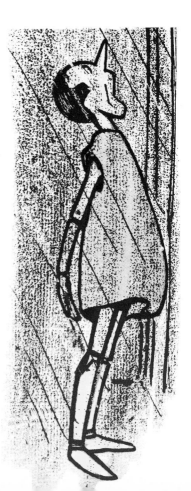

"Dear little Snail," cried Pinocchio from the street. "I have been waiting two hours for you! And two hours on a dreadful night like this are as long as two years. Hurry, please!"

"My boy," answered the Snail in a calm, peaceful voice, "my dear boy, I am a snail and snails are never in a hurry." And the window closed.

A few minutes later midnight struck; then one o'clock—two o'clock. And the door still remained closed!

Then Pinocchio, losing all patience, grabbed the knocker with both hands, fully determined to awaken the whole house and street with it. As soon as he touched the knocker, however, it became an eel and wiggled away into the darkness.

"Really?" cried Pinocchio, blind with rage. "If the knocker is gone, I can still use my feet."

He stepped back and gave the door a most solemn kick. He kicked so hard that his foot went straight through the door and his leg followed almost to the knee. No matter how he pulled and tugged, he could not pull it out. There he stayed as if nailed to the door.

Poor Pinocchio! The rest of the night he had to spend with one foot through the door and the other one in the air.

As dawn was breaking, the

door finally opened. That brave little animal, the Snail, had taken exactly nine hours to go from the fourth floor to the street. How she must have raced!

"What are you doing with your foot through the door?" she asked the Marionette, laughing.

"It was a misfortune. Won't you try, pretty little Snail, to free me from this terrible torture?"

"My boy, we need a carpenter here and I have never been one."

"Ask the Fairy to help me!"

"The Fairy is asleep and does not want to be disturbed."

"But what do you want me to do, nailed to the door like this?"

"Enjoy yourself counting the ants which are passing by."

"Bring me something to eat, at least, for I am faint with hunger."

"Immediately!"

In fact, after three hours and a half, Pinocchio saw her return with a silver tray on her head. On the tray there was bread, roast chicken, fruit.

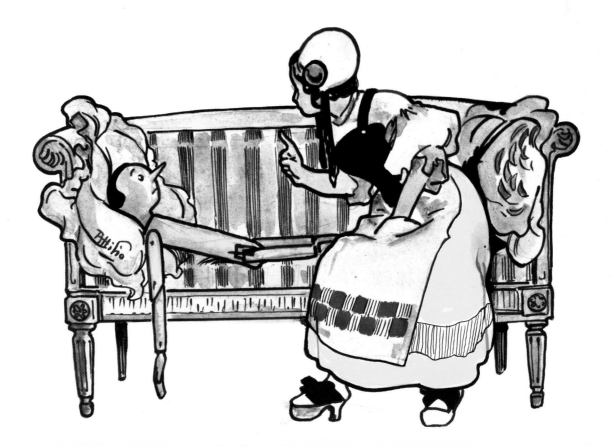

"Here is the breakfast the Fairy sends to you," said the Snail.

At the sight of all these good things, the Marionette felt much better.

What was his disgust, however, when on tasting the food, he found the bread to be made of chalk, the chicken of cardboard, and the brilliant fruit of colored alabaster!

He wanted to cry, he wanted to give himself up to despair, he wanted to throw away the tray and all that was on it. Instead, either from pain or weakness, he fell to the floor in a dead faint.

When he regained his senses, he found himself stretched out on a sofa and the Fairy was seated near him.

"This time also I forgive you," said the Fairy to him. "But be careful not to get into mischief again."

Pinocchio promised to study and to behave himself. And he kept his word for the remainder of the year. At the end of it, he passed first in all his examinations, and his report was so good that the Fairy said to him happily:

"Tomorrow your wish will come true."

"And what is it?"

"Tomorrow you will cease to be a Marionette and will become a real boy."

Pinocchio was beside himself with joy. All his friends and schoolmates must be invited to celebrate the great event! The Fairy promised to prepare two hundred cups of coffee-and-milk and four hundred slices of toast buttered on both sides.

The day promised to be a very gay and happy one, but—

Unluckily, in a Marionette's life there's always a *but* which is apt to spoil everything.

CHAPTER 30

*Pinocchio, instead of becoming a boy,
runs away to the Land of Toys with
his friend, Lamp-Wick.*

Coming at last out of the surprise into which the Fairy's words had thrown him, Pinocchio asked for permission to give out the invitations.

"Indeed, you may invite your friends to tomorrow's party. Only remember to return home before dark. Do you understand?"

"I'll be back in one hour without fail," answered the Marionette.

"Take care, Pinocchio! Boys give promises very easily, but they as easily forget them."

"But I am not like those others. When I give my word I keep it."

"We shall see. In case you do disobey, you will be the one to suffer, not anyone else."

"Why?"

"Because boys who do not listen to their elders always come to grief."

"I certainly have," said Pinocchio, "but from now on, I obey."

"We shall see if you are telling the truth."

Without adding another word, the Marionette bade the good Fairy good-by, and singing and dancing, he left the house.

In a little more than an hour, all his friends were invited. Some accepted quickly and gladly. Others had to be coaxed, but when they heard that the toast was to be buttered on both sides, they all ended by accepting the invitation with the words, "We'll come to please you."

Now it must be known that, among all his friends, Pinocchio had one whom he loved most of all. The boy's real name was Romeo, but everyone called him Lamp-Wick, for he was long and thin and had a woebegone look about him.

Lamp-Wick was the laziest boy in the school and the biggest mischief-maker, but Pinocchio loved him dearly.

That day, he went straight to his friend's house to invite him to the party, but Lamp-Wick was not at home. He went a second time, and again a third, but still without success.

Where could he be? Pinocchio searched here and there and everywhere, and finally discovered him hiding near a farmer's wagon.

"What are you doing there?" asked Pinocchio, running up to him.

"I am waiting for midnight to strike to go—"

"Where?"

"Far, far away!"

"And I have gone to your house three times to look for you!"

"What did you want from me?"

"Haven't you heard the news? Don't you know what good luck is mine?"

"What is it?"

"Tomorrow I end my days as a Marionette and become a boy, like you and all my other friends."

"May it bring you luck!"

"Shall I see you at my party tomorrow?"

"But I'm telling you that I go tonight."

"At what time?"

"At midnight."

"And where are you going?"

"To a real country—the best in the world—a wonderful place!"

"What is it called?"

"It is called the Land of Toys. Why don't you come, too?"

"I? Oh, no!"

"You are making a big mistake, Pinocchio. Believe me, if you don't come, you'll be sorry. Where can you find a place that will agree better with you and me? No schools, no teachers, no books! In that blessed place there is no such thing as study. Here, it is only on Thursdays that we have no school. In the Land of Toys, every day, except Sunday, is a Thursday. Vacation begins on the first of January and ends on the last

237

day of December. That is the place for me! All countries should be like it! How happy we should all be!"

"But how does one spend the day in the Land of Toys?"

"Days are spent in play and enjoyment from morn till night. At night one goes to bed, and next morning, the good times begin all over again. What do you think of it?"

"H'm—!" said Pinocchio, nodding his wooden head, as if to say, "It's the kind of life which would agree with me perfectly."

"Do you want to go with me, then? Yes or no? You must make up your mind."

"No, no, and again no! I promised my kind Fairy to become a good boy, and I want to keep my word. Just see: The sun is setting and I must leave you and run. Good-by and good luck to you!"

"Where are you going in such a hurry?"

"Home. My good Fairy wants me to return home before night."

"Wait two minutes more."

"It's too late!"

"Only two minutes."

"And if the Fairy scolds me?"

"Let her scold. After she gets tired, she will stop," said Lamp-Wick.

"Are you going alone or with others?"

"Alone? There will be more than a hundred of us!"

"Will you walk?"

"At midnight the wagon passes here that is to take us within the boundaries of that marvelous country."

"How I wish midnight would strike!"

"Why?"

"To see you all set out together."

"Stay here a while longer and you will see us!"

"No, no. I want to return home."

"Wait two more minutes."

"I have waited too long as it is. The Fairy will be worried."

"Poor Fairy! Is she afraid the bats will eat you up?"

"Listen, Lamp-Wick," said the Marionette, "are you really sure that there are no schools in the Land of Toys?"

"Not even the shadow of one."

"Not even one teacher?"

"Not one."

"And one does not have to study?"

"Never, never, never!"

"What a great land!" said Pinocchio, feeling his mouth water. "What a beautiful land! I have never been there, but I can well imagine it."

"Why don't you come, too?"

"It is useless for you to tempt me! I told you I promised my good Fairy to behave myself, and I am going to keep my word."

"Good-by, then, and remember me to the grammar schools, to the high schools, and even to the colleges if you meet them on the way."

"Good-by, Lamp-Wick. Have a pleasant trip, enjoy yourself, and remember your friends once in a while."

With these words, the Marionette started on his way home. Turning once more to his friend, he asked him:

"But are you sure that, in that country, each week is composed of six Thursdays and one Sunday?"

"Very sure!"

"And that vacation begins on the first of January and ends on the thirty-first of December?"

"Very, very sure!"

"What a great country!" repeated Pinocchio, puzzled as to what to do.

Then, in sudden determination, he said hurriedly:

"Good-by for the last time, and good luck."

"Good-by."

"How soon will you go?"

"Within two hours."

"What a pity! If it were only one hour, I might wait for you."

"And the Fairy?"

"By this time I'm late, and one hour more or less makes very little difference."

"Poor Pinocchio! And if the Fairy scolds you?"

"Oh, I'll let her scold. After she gets tired, she will stop."

In the meantime, the night became darker and darker. All at once in the distance a small light flickered. A queer sound could be heard, soft as a little bell, and faint and muffled like the buzz of a far-away mosquito.

"There it is!" cried Lamp-Wick, jumping to his feet.

"What?" whispered Pinocchio.

"The wagon which is coming to get me. For the last time, are you coming or not?"

"But is it really true that in that country boys never have to study?"

"Never, never, never!"

"What a wonderful, beautiful, marvelous country! Oh—h—h!!"

CHAPTER 31

*After five months
of play, Pinocchio
wakes up one fine
morning and finds
a great surprise
awaiting him.*

Finally the wagon arrived. It made no noise, for its wheels were bound with straw and rags.

It was drawn by twelve pairs of donkeys, all of the same size, but all of different colors. Some were gray, others white, and still others a mixture of brown and black. Here and there were a few with large yellow and blue stripes.

The strangest thing of all was that those twenty-four donkeys, instead of being iron-shod like any other beast of burden, had on their feet laced shoes made of leather, just like the ones boys wear.

And the driver of the wagon?

Imagine to yourselves a little, fat man, much wider than he was long, round and shiny as a ball of butter, with a face beaming like an apple, a little mouth that always smiled, and a voice small and wheedling like that of a cat begging for food.

No sooner did any boy see him than he fell in love with him, and nothing satisfied him but to be allowed to ride in his wagon to that lovely place called the Land of Toys.

In fact the wagon was so closely packed with boys of all ages that it looked like a box of sardines. They were uncomfortable, they were piled one on top of the other, they could hardly breathe; yet not one word of complaint was heard. The thought that in a few hours they would reach a country where there were no schools, no books, no teachers, made these boys so happy that they felt neither hunger, nor thirst, nor sleep, nor discomfort.

No sooner had the wagon stopped than the little fat man turned to Lamp-Wick. With bows and smiles, he asked in a wheedling tone:

"Tell me, my fine boy, do you also want to come to my wonderful country?"

"Indeed I do."

"But I warn you, my little dear, there's no more room in the wagon. It is full."

"Never mind," answered Lamp-Wick. "If there's no room inside, I can sit on the top of the coach."

And with one leap, he perched himself there.

"What about you, my love?" asked the Little Man, turning politely to Pinocchio. "What are you going to do? Will you come with us, or do you stay here?"

"I stay here," answered Pinocchio. "I want to return home, as I prefer to study and to succeed in life."

"May that bring you luck!"

"Pinocchio!" Lamp-Wick called out. "Listen to me. Come with us and we'll always be happy."

"No, no, no!"

"Come with us and we'll always be happy," cried four other voices from the wagon.

"Come with us and we'll always be happy," shouted the one hundred and more boys in the wagon, all together.

"And if I go with you, what will my good Fairy say?" asked the Marionette, who was beginning to waver and weaken in his good resolutions.

"Don't worry so much. Only think that we are going to a land where we shall be allowed to make all the racket we like from morning till night."

Pinocchio did not answer, but sighed deeply once—twice—a third time. Finally, he said:

"Make room for me. I want to go, too!"

"The seats are all filled," answered the Little Man, "but to show you how much I think of you, take my place as coachman."

"And you?"

"I'll walk."

"No, indeed. I could not permit such a thing. I much prefer riding one of these donkeys," cried Pinocchio.

No sooner said than done. He approached the first donkey and tried to mount it. But the little animal turned suddenly and gave him such a terrible kick in the stomach that Pinocchio was thrown to the ground and fell with his legs in the air.

At this unlooked-for entertainment, the whole company of runaways laughed uproariously.

The little fat man did not laugh. He went up to the rebellious animal, and, still smiling, bent over him lovingly and bit off half of his right ear.

In the meantime, Pinocchio lifted himself up from the ground, and with one leap landed on the donkey's back. The leap was so well taken that all the boys shouted, "Hurrah for Pinocchio!" and clapped their hands in hearty applause.

Suddenly the little donkey gave a kick with his two hind feet and, at this unexpected move, the poor Marionette found himself once again sprawling right in the middle of the road.

Again the boys shouted with laughter. But the Little Man, instead of laughing, became so loving toward the little animal that, with another kiss, he bit off half of his left ear.

"You can mount now, my boy," he then said to Pinocchio. "Have no fear. That donkey was worried about something, but I have spoken to him and now he seems quiet and reasonable."

Pinocchio mounted and the wagon started on its way. While the donkeys galloped along the stony road, the Marionette fancied he heard a very quiet voice whispering to him:

"Poor silly! You have done as you wished. But you are going to be a sorry boy before very long."

Pinocchio, greatly frightened, looked about him to see whence the words had come, but he saw no one. The donkeys galloped, the wagon rolled on smoothly, the boys slept (Lamp-Wick snored like a dormouse) and the little, fat driver sang sleepily between his teeth:

"All night long they sleep,
But never any sleep have I."

After a mile or so, Pinocchio again heard the same faint voice whispering: "Remember, little simpleton! Boys who stop studying and turn their backs upon books and schools and teachers in order to give all their time to nonsense and pleasure, sooner or later come to grief. Oh, how well I know this! How well I can prove it to you! The day will come when you will weep bitterly, even as

I am weeping now—but it will be too late!"

At these whispered words, the Marionette grew more and more frightened. He jumped to the ground, ran up to the donkey on whose back he had been riding, and taking his nose in his hands, looked at him. Think how great was his surprise when he saw that the donkey was weeping—weeping just like a boy!

"Hey, Mr. Driver!" cried the Marionette. "Do you know what strange thing is happening here! This donkey weeps."

"Let him weep. When he gets married, he will have time to laugh."

"Have you perhaps taught him to speak?"

"No, he learned to mumble a few words when he lived for three years with a band of trained dogs."

"Poor beast!"

"Come, come," said the Little Man, "do not lose time over a donkey that can weep. Mount quickly and let us go. The night is cool and the road is long."

Pinocchio obeyed without another word. The wagon started again. Toward dawn the next morning they finally reached that much-longed-for country, the Land of Toys.

This great land was entirely different from any other place in the world. Its population, large though it was, was composed wholly of boys. The oldest were about fourteen years of age, the youngest, eight. In the street, there was such a racket, such shouting, such blowing of trumpets, that it was deafening. Everywhere groups of boys were gathered together. Some played at marbles, at hopscotch, at ball. Others rode on bicycles or on wooden horses. Some played at blindman's bluff, others at tag. Here a group played circus, there another sang and recited. A few turned somersaults, others walked on their hands with their feet in the air. Generals in full uniform leading regiments of cardboard soldiers passed by. Laughter, shrieks, howls, catcalls, hand-clapping followed this parade. One boy made a noise like a hen, another like a rooster, and a third imitated a lion in his den. All together they created such a pandemonium that it would have been necessary for you to put cotton in your ears. The squares were filled with small wooden theaters, overflowing with boys from morning till night, and on the walls of the houses, written with charcoal, were words like these: *Hurrah for the Land of Toys! Down with arithmetic! No more school!*

As soon as they had set foot in that land, Pinocchio, Lamp-Wick, and all the other boys who had traveled with them started out on a tour of investigation. They wandered everywhere, they looked into every nook and corner, house and theater. They became everybody's friend. Who could be happier than they?

What with entertainments and parties, the hours, the days, the weeks passed like lightning.

"Oh, what a beautiful life this is!" said Pinocchio each time that, by chance, he met his friend Lamp-Wick.

"Was I right or wrong?" answered Lamp-Wick. "And to think you did not want to come! To think that even yesterday the idea came into your head to return home to see your Fairy and to start studying again! If today you are free from pencils and books and school, you owe it to me, to my advice, to my care. Do you admit it? Only true friends count, after all."

"It's true, Lamp-Wick, it's true. If today I am a really happy boy, it is all because of you. And to think that the teacher, when speaking of you, used to say, 'Do not go with that Lamp-Wick! He is a bad companion and someday he will lead you astray.'"

"Poor teacher!" answered the other, nodding his head. "Indeed I know how much he disliked me and how he enjoyed speaking ill of me. But I am of a generous nature, and I gladly forgive him."

"Great soul!" said Pinocchio, fondly embracing his friend.

Five months passed and the boys continued playing and enjoying themselves from morn till night, without ever seeing a book, or a desk, or a school. But, my children, there came a morning when Pinocchio awoke and found a great surprise awaiting him, a surprise which made him feel very unhappy, as you shall see.

CHAPTER 32

Pinocchio's ears become like those of a Donkey. In a little while he changes into a real Donkey and begins to bray.

Everyone, at one time or another, has found some surprise awaiting him. Of the kind which Pinocchio had on that eventful morning of his life, there are but few.

What was it? I will tell you, my dear little readers. On awakening, Pinocchio put his hand up to his head and there he found —

Guess!

He found that, during the night, his ears had grown at least ten full inches!

You must know that the Marionette, even from his birth, had very small ears, so small indeed that to the naked eye they could hardly be seen. Fancy how he felt when he noticed that overnight those two dainty organs had become as long as shoe brushes!

He went in search of a mirror, but not finding any, he just filled a basin with water and looked at himself. There he saw what he never could have wished to see. His manly figure was adorned and enriched by a beautiful pair of donkey's ears.

I leave you to think of the terrible grief, the shame, the despair of the poor Marionette.

He began to cry, to scream, to knock his head against the wall, but the more he shrieked, the longer and the more hairy grew his ears.

At those piercing shrieks, a Dormouse came into the room, a fat little Dormouse, who lived upstairs. Seeing Pinocchio so grief-stricken, she asked him anxiously:

"What is the matter, dear little neighbor?"

"I am sick, my little Dormouse, very, very sick—and from an illness which frightens me! Do you understand how to feel the pulse?"

"A little."

"Feel mine then and tell me if I have a fever."

The Dormouse took Pinocchio's wrist between her paws and, after a few minutes, looked up at him sorrowfully and said: "My friend, I am sorry, but I must give you some very sad news."

"What is it?"

"You have a very bad fever."

"But what fever is it?"

"The donkey fever."

"I don't know anything about that fever," answered the Marionette, beginning to understand even too well what was happening to him.

"Then I will tell you all about it," said the Dormouse. "Know then that, within two or three hours, you will no longer be a Marionette, nor a boy."

"What shall I be?"

"Within two or three hours you will become a real donkey, just like the ones that pull the fruit carts to market."

"Oh, what have I done? What have I done?" cried Pinocchio, grasping his two long ears in his hands and pulling and tugging at them angrily, just as if they belonged to another.

"My dear boy," answered the Dormouse to cheer him up a bit, "why worry now? What is done cannot be undone, you know. Fate has decreed that all lazy boys who come to hate books and schools and teachers and spend all their days with toys and games must sooner or later turn into donkeys."

"But is it really so?" asked the Marionette, sobbing bitterly.

"I am sorry to say it is. And tears now are useless. You should have thought of all this before."

"But the fault is not mine. Believe me, little Dormouse, the fault is all Lamp-Wick's."

"And who is this Lamp-Wick?"

"A classmate of mine. I wanted to return home. I wanted to be obedient. I wanted to study and

to succeed in school, but Lamp-Wick said to me, 'Why do you want to waste your time studying? Why do you want to go to school? Come with me to the Land of Toys. There we'll never study again. There we can enjoy ourselves and be happy from morn till night.'"

"And why did you follow the advice of that false friend?"

"Why? Because, my dear little Dormouse, I am a heedless Marionette—heedless and heartless. Oh! If I had only had a bit of heart, I should never have abandoned that good Fairy, who loved me so well and who has been so kind to me! And by this time, I should no longer be a Marionette. I should have become a real boy, like all these friends of mine! Oh, if I meet Lamp-Wick I am going to tell him what I think of him—and more, too!"

After this long speech, Pinocchio walked to the door of the room. But when he reached it, remembering his donkey ears, he felt ashamed to show them to the public and turned back. He took a large cotton bag from a shelf, put it on his head, and pulled it far down to his very nose.

Thus adorned, he went out. He looked for Lamp-Wick everywhere, along the streets, in the squares, inside the theaters, everywhere; but he was not to be found. He asked everyone whom he met about him, but no one had seen him. In desperation, he returned home and knocked at the door.

"Who is it?" asked Lamp-Wick from within.

258

"It is I!" answered the Marionette.

"Wait a minute."

After a full half hour the door opened. Another surprise awaited Pinocchio! There in the room stood his friend, with a large cotton bag on his head, pulled far down to his very nose.

At the sight of that bag, Pinocchio felt slightly happier and thought to himself:

"My friend must be suffering from the same sickness that I am! I wonder if he, too, has donkey fever?"

But pretending he had seen nothing, he asked with a smile:

"How are you, my dear Lamp-Wick?"

"Very well. Like a mouse in a Parmesan cheese."

"Is that really true?"

"Why should I lie to you?"

"I beg your pardon, my friend, but why then are you wearing that cotton bag over your ears?"

"The doctor has ordered it because one of my knees hurts. And you, dear Marionette, why are you wearing that cotton bag down to your nose?"

"The doctor has ordered it because I have bruised my foot."

"Oh, my poor Pinocchio!"

"Oh, my poor Lamp-Wick!"

An embarrassingly long silence followed these words, during which time the two friends looked at each other in a mocking way.

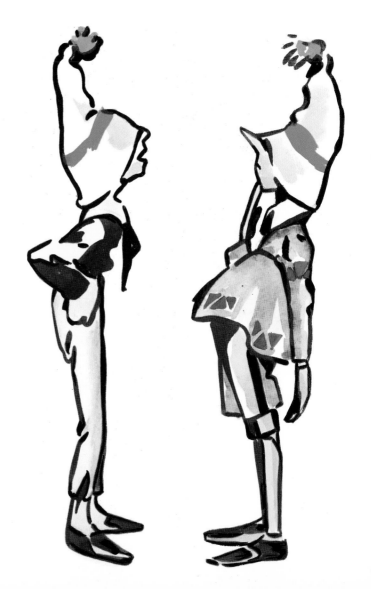

Finally the Marionette, in a voice sweet as honey and soft as a flute, said to his companion:

"Tell me, Lamp-Wick, dear friend, have you ever suffered from an earache?"

"Never! And you?"

"Never! Still, since this morning my ear has been torturing me."

"So has mine."

"Yours, too? And which ear is it?"

"Both of them. And yours?"

"Both of them, too. I wonder if it could be the same sickness."

"I'm afraid it is."

"Will you do me a favor, Lamp-Wick?"

"Gladly! With my whole heart."

"Will you let me see your ears?"

"Why not? But before I show you mine, I want to see yours, dear Pinocchio."

"No. You must show yours first."

"No, my dear! Yours first, then mine."

"Well, then," said the Marionette, "let us make a contract."

"Let's hear the contract!"

"Let us take off our caps together. All right?"

"All right."

"Ready then!"

Pinocchio began to count, "One! Two! Three!"

At the word "Three!" the two boys pulled off their caps and threw them high in air.

And then a scene took place which is hard to believe, but it is all too true. The Marionette and his friend, Lamp-Wick, when they saw each other both stricken by the same misfortune, instead of feeling sorrowful and ashamed, began to poke fun at each other, and after much nonsense, they ended by bursting out into hearty laughter.

They laughed and laughed, and laughed again—laughed till they ached—laughed till they cried.

But all of a sudden Lamp-Wick stopped laughing. He tottered and almost fell. Pale as a ghost, he turned to Pinocchio and said:

"Help, help, Pinocchio!"

"What is the matter?"

"Oh, help me! I can no longer stand up."

"I can't either," cried Pinocchio; and his laughter turned to tears as he stumbled about helplessly.

They had hardly finished speaking, when both of them fell on all fours and began running and jumping around the room. As they ran, their arms turned into legs, their faces lengthened into snouts and their backs became covered with long gray hairs.

This was humiliation enough, but the most horrible moment was the one in which the two poor creatures felt their tails appear. Overcome with shame and grief, they tried to cry and bemoan their fate.

But what is done can't be undone! Instead of moans and cries, they burst forth into loud donkey brays, which sounded very much like, "Haw! Haw! Haw!"

At that moment, a loud knocking was heard at the door and a voice called to them:

"Open! I am the Little Man, the driver of the wagon which brought you here. Open, I say, or beware!"

CHAPTER 33

Pinocchio, having become a Donkey, is bought by the owner of a Circus, who wants to teach him to do tricks. The Donkey becomes lame and is sold to a man who wants to use his skin for a drumhead.

GREAT SPECTACLE TONIGHT

LEAPS AND EXERCISES BY THE
GREAT ARTISTS
AND THE FAMOUS HORSES
of the
COMPANY

First Public Appearance
of the
FAMOUS DONKEY
called

PINOCCHIO

THE STAR OF THE DANCE

Very sad and downcast were the two poor little fellows as they stood and looked at each other. Outside the room, the Little Man grew more and more impatient, and finally gave the door such a violent kick that it flew open. With his usual sweet smile on his lips, he looked at Pinocchio and Lamp-Wick and said to them:

"Fine work, boys! You have brayed well, so well that I recognized your voices immediately, and here I am."

On hearing this, the two Donkeys bowed their heads in shame, dropped their ears, and put their tails between their legs.

At first, the Little Man petted and caressed them and smoothed down their hairy coats. Then he took out a currycomb and worked over them till they shone like glass. Satisfied with the looks of the two little animals, he bridled them and took them to a market place far away from the Land of Toys, in the hope of selling them at a good price.

In fact, he did not have to wait very long for an offer. Lamp-Wick was bought by a farmer whose donkey had died the day before. Pinocchio went to the owner of a circus, who wanted to teach him to do tricks for his audiences.

And now do you understand what the Little Man's profession was? This horrid little being, whose face shone with kindness, went about the world looking for boys. Lazy boys, boys who hated books, boys who wanted to run away from home, boys who were tired of school—all these were his joy and his fortune. He took them with him to the Land of Toys and let them enjoy themselves to their heart's content. When, after months of all play and no work, they became little donkeys, he sold them on the market place. In a few years, he had become a millionaire.

What happened to Lamp-Wick? My dear children, I do not know. Pinocchio, I can tell you, met with great hardships even from the first day.

After putting him in a stable, his new master filled his manger with straw, but Pinocchio, after tasting a mouthful, spat it out.

Then the man filled the manger with hay. But Pinocchio did not like that any better.

"Ah, you don't like hay either?" he cried angrily. "Wait, my pretty Donkey, I'll teach you not to be so particular."

Without more ado, he took a whip and gave the Donkey a hearty blow across the legs.

Pinocchio screamed with pain and as he screamed he brayed:

"Haw! Haw! Haw! I can't digest straw!"

"Then eat the hay!" answered his master, who understood the Donkey perfectly.

"Haw! Haw! Haw! Hay gives me a headache!"

"Do you pretend, by any chance, that I should feed you duck or chicken?" asked the man again, and, angrier than ever, he gave poor Pinocchio another lashing.

At that second beating, Pinocchio became very quiet and said no more.

After that, the door of the stable was closed and he was left alone. It was many hours since he had eaten anything and he started to yawn from hunger. As he yawned, he opened a mouth as big as an oven.

Finally, not finding anything else in the manger, he tasted the hay. After tasting it, he chewed it well, closed his eyes, and swallowed it.

"This hay is not bad," he said to himself. "But how much happier I should be if I had studied! Just now, instead of hay, I should be eating some good bread and butter. Patience!"

Next morning, when he awoke, Pinocchio looked in the manger for more hay, but it was all gone. He had eaten it all during the night.

He tried the straw, but, as he chewed away at it, he noticed to his great disappointment that it tasted neither like rice nor like macaroni.

"Patience!" he repeated as he chewed. "If only my misfortune might serve as a lesson to disobedient boys who refuse to study! Patience! Have patience!"

"Patience indeed!" shouted his master just then, as he came into the stable. "Do you think, perhaps, my little Donkey, that I have brought you here only to give you food and drink? Oh, no! You are to help me earn some fine gold pieces, do you hear? Come along, now. I am going to teach you to jump and bow, to dance a waltz and a polka, and even to stand on your head."

Poor Pinocchio, whether he liked it or not, had to learn all these wonderful things; but it took him three long months and cost him many, many lashings before he was pronounced perfect.

The day came at last when Pinocchio's master was able to announce an extraordinary performance. The announcements, posted all around the town, and written in large letters, read thus:

GREAT SPECTACLE
TONIGHT

LEAPS AND EXERCISES BY THE
GREAT ARTISTS
AND THE FAMOUS HORSES
of the
COMPANY

First Public Appearance
of the
FAMOUS DONKEY
called

PINOCCHIO
THE STAR OF THE DANCE

*The Theater will be
as Light as Day*

That night, as you can well imagine, the theater was filled to overflowing one hour before the show was scheduled to start.

Not an orchestra chair could be had, not a balcony seat, nor a gallery seat; not even for their weight in gold.

The place swarmed with boys and girls of all ages and sizes, wriggling and dancing about in a fever of impatience to see the famous Donkey dance.

When the first part of the performance was over, the Owner and Manager of the circus, in a black coat, white knee breeches, and patent leather boots, presented himself to the public and in a loud, pompous voice made the following announcement:

"Most honored friends, Gentlemen and Ladies!

"Your humble servant, the Manager of this theater, presents himself before you tonight in order to introduce to you the greatest, the most famous Donkey in the world, a Donkey that has had the great honor in his short life of performing before the kings and queens and emperors of all the great courts of Europe.

"We thank you for your attention!"

This speech was greeted by much laughter and applause. And the applause grew to a roar when Pinocchio, the famous Donkey, appeared in the circus ring. He was handsomely arrayed. A new bridle of shining leather with buckles of polished brass was on his back; two white camellias were tied to his ears; ribbons and tassels of red silk adorned his mane, which was divided into many curls. A great sash of gold and silver was fastened around his waist and his tail was decorated with ribbons of many brilliant colors. He was a handsome Donkey indeed!

The Manager, when introducing him to the public, added these words:

"Most honored audience! I shall not take your time tonight to

tell you of the great difficulties which I have encountered while trying to tame this animal, since I found him in the wilds of Africa. Observe, I beg of you, the savage look of his eye. All the means used by centuries of civilization in subduing wild beasts failed in this case. I had finally to resort to the gentle language of the whip in order to bring him to my will. With all my kindness, however, I never succeeded in gaining my Donkey's love. He is still today as savage as the day I found him. He still fears and hates me. But I have found in him one great redeeming feature. Do you see this little bump on his forehead? It is this bump which gives him his great talent of dancing and using his feet as nimbly as a human being. Admire him, O signori, and enjoy yourselves. I let you, now, be the judges of my success as a teacher of animals. Before I leave you, I wish to state that there will be another performance tomorrow night. If the weather threatens rain, the great spectacle will take place at eleven o'clock in the morning."

The Manager bowed and then turned to Pinocchio and said: "Ready, Pinocchio! Before starting your performance, salute your audience!"

Pinocchio obediently bent his two knees to the ground and remained kneeling until the Manager, with the crack of the whip, cried sharply: "Walk!"

The Donkey lifted himself on his four feet and walked around the ring. A few minutes passed and again the voice of the Manager called:

"Quickstep!" and Pinocchio obediently changed his step.

"Gallop!" and Pinocchio galloped.

"Full speed!" and Pinocchio ran as fast as he could. As he ran the master raised his arm and a pistol shot rang in the air.

At the shot, the little Donkey fell to the ground as if he were really dead.

A shower of applause greeted the Donkey as he arose to his feet. Cries and shouts and handclappings were heard on all sides.

At all that noise, Pinocchio lifted his head and raised his eyes. There, in front of him, in a box sat a beautiful woman. Around her neck she wore a long gold chain, from which hung a large medallion. On the medallion was painted the picture of a Marionette.

"That picture is of me! That beautiful lady is my Fairy!" said Pinocchio to himself, recognizing her. He felt so happy that he tried his best to cry out:

"Oh, my Fairy! My own Fairy!"

But instead of words, a loud braying was heard in the theater, so loud and so long that all the spectators—men, women, and children, but especially the children—burst out laughing.

Then, in order to teach the Donkey that it was not good manners to bray before the public, the Manager hit him on the nose with the handle of the whip.

The poor little Donkey stuck out a long tongue and licked his nose for a long time in an effort to take away the pain.

And what was his grief when, on looking up toward the boxes, he saw that the Fairy had disappeared!

He felt himself fainting, his eyes filled with tears, and he wept bitterly. No one knew it, however, least of all the Manager, who, cracking his whip, cried out:

"Bravo, Pinocchio! Now show us how gracefully you can jump through the rings."

Pinocchio tried two or three times, but each time he came near the ring, he found it more to his taste to go under it. The fourth time, at a look from his master he leaped through it, but as he did so his hind legs caught in the ring and he fell to the floor in a heap.

When he got up, he was lame and could hardly limp as far as the stable.

"Pinocchio! We want Pinocchio! We want the little Donkey!" cried the boys from the orchestra, saddened by the accident.

No one saw Pinocchio again that evening.

The next morning the veterinarian—that is, the animal doctor—declared that he would be lame for the rest of his life.

"What do I want with a lame donkey?" said the Manager to the stableboy. "Take him to the market and sell him."

When they reached the square, a buyer was soon found.

"How much do you ask for that little lame Donkey?" he asked.

"Four dollars."

"I'll give you four cents. Don't think I'm buying him for work. I want only his skin. It looks very tough and I can use it to make myself a drumhead. I belong to a musical band in my village and I need a drum."

I leave it to you, my dear children, to picture to yourself the great pleasure with which Pinocchio heard that he was to become a drumhead!

As soon as the buyer had paid the four cents, the Donkey changed hands. His new owner took him to a high cliff overlooking the sea, put a stone around his neck, tied a rope to one of his hind feet, gave him a push, and threw him into the water.

Pinocchio sank immediately. And his new master sat on the cliff waiting for him to drown, so as to skin him and make himself a drumhead.

CHAPTER 34

*Pinocchio is thrown into the sea, eaten
by fishes, and becomes a Marionette
once more. As he swims to land, he is
swallowed by the Terrible Shark.*

Down into the sea, deeper and deeper, sank Pinocchio and, finally, after fifty minutes of waiting, the man on the cliff said to himself:

"By this time my poor little lame Donkey must be drowned. Up with him and then I can get to work on my beautiful drum."

He pulled the rope which he had tied to Pinocchio's leg—pulled and pulled and pulled and, at last, he saw appear on the surface of the water—Can you guess what? Instead of a dead donkey, he saw a very much alive Marionette, wriggling and squirming like an eel.

Seeing that wooden Marionette, the poor man thought he was dreaming and sat there with his mouth wide open and his eyes popping out of his head.

Gathering his wits together, he said:

"And the Donkey I threw into the sea?"

"I am that Donkey," answered the Marionette, laughing.

"You?"

"I."

"Ah, you little cheat! Are you poking fun at me?"

"Poking fun at you? Not at all, dear Master. I am talking seriously."

"But, then, how is it that you, who a few minutes ago were a donkey, are now standing before me a wooden Marionette?"

"It may be the effect of salt water. The sea is fond of playing these tricks."

"Be careful, Marionette, be careful! Don't laugh at me! Woe be to you, if I lose my patience!"

"Well, then, my Master, do you want to know my whole story? Untie my leg and I can tell it to you better."

The old fellow, curious to know the true story of the Marionette's life, immediately untied the rope which held his foot. Pinocchio, feeling free as a bird of the air, began his tale:

"Know, then, that, once upon a time, I was a wooden Marionette, just as I am today. One day I was about to become a boy, a real boy, but on account of my laziness and my hatred of books, and because I listened to bad companions, I ran away from home. One beautiful morning, I awoke to find myself changed into a donkey—long ears, gray coat, even a tail! What a shameful day for me! I hope you will never experience one like it, dear Master. I was taken to the fair and sold to a Circus Owner, who tried to make me dance and jump through the rings. One night, during a performance, I had a bad fall and became lame. Not knowing what to do with a lame donkey, the Circus Owner sent me to the market place and you bought me."

"Indeed I did! And I paid four cents for you. Now who will return my money to me?"

"But why did you buy me? You bought me to do me harm—to kill me—to make a drumhead out of me!"

"Indeed I did! And now where shall I find another skin?"

"Never mind, dear Master. There are so many donkeys in this world."

"Tell me, impudent little rogue, does your story end here?"

"One more word," answered the Marionette, "and I am through. After buying me, you brought me here to kill me. But feeling sorry for me, you tied a stone to my neck and threw me to the bottom of the sea. That was very good and kind of you to want me to suffer as little as possible and I shall remember you always. And now my Fairy will take care of me, even if you—"

"Your Fairy? Who is she?"

"She is my mother, and, like all other mothers who love their children, she never loses sight of me, even though I do not deserve it. And today this good Fairy of mine, as soon as she saw me in danger of drowning, sent a thousand fishes to the spot where I lay. They thought I was really a dead donkey and began to eat me. What great bites they took! One ate my ears, another my nose,

a third my neck and my mane. Some went at my legs and some at my back, and among the others, there was one tiny fish so gentle and polite that he did me the great favor of eating even my tail."

"From now on," said the man, horrified, "I swear I shall never again taste fish. How I should enjoy opening a mullet or a white-fish just to find there the tail of a dead donkey!"

"I think as you do," answered the Marionette, laughing. "Still, you must know that when the fish finished eating my donkey coat, which covered me from head to foot, they naturally came to the bones—or rather, in my case, to the wood, for as you know, I am made of very hard wood. After the first few bites, those greedy fish found out that the wood was not good for their teeth, and, afraid of indigestion, they turned and ran here and there without saying good-by or even as much as thank you to me. Here, dear Master, you have my story. You know now why you found a Marionette and not a dead donkey when you pulled me out of the water."

"I laugh at your story!" cried the man angrily. "I know that I spent four cents to get you and I want my money back. Do you know what I can do? I am going to take you to the market once more and sell you as dry firewood."

"Very well, sell me. I am satisfied," said Pinocchio. But as he spoke, he gave a quick leap and dived into the sea. Swimming away as fast as he could, he cried out, laughing:

"Good-by, Master. If you ever need a skin for your drum, re-member me."

He swam on and on. After a while, he turned around again and called louder than before:

"Good-by, Master. If you ever need a piece of good dry fire-wood, remember me."

In a few seconds he had gone so far he could hardly be seen. All that could be seen of him was a very small black dot moving swiftly on the blue surface of the water, a little black dot which

now and then lifted a leg or an arm in the air. One would have thought that Pinocchio had turned into a porpoise playing in the sun.

After swimming for a long time, Pinocchio saw a large rock in the middle of the sea, a rock as white as marble. High on the rock stood a little Goat bleating and calling and beckoning to the Marionette to come to her.

There was something very strange about that little goat. Her coat was not white or black or brown as that of any other goat, but azure, a deep brilliant color that reminded one of the hair of the lovely maiden.

Pinocchio's heart beat fast, and then faster and faster. He redoubled his efforts and swam as hard as he could toward the white rock. He was almost halfway over, when suddenly a horrible sea monster stuck its head out of the water, an enormous head with a huge mouth, wide open, showing three rows of gleaming teeth, the mere sight of which would have filled you with fear.

Do you know what it was?

That sea monster was no other than the enormous Shark, which has often been mentioned in this story and which, on account of its cruelty, had been nicknamed "The Attila of the Sea" by both fish and fishermen.

Poor Pinocchio! The sight of that monster frightened him almost to death! He tried to swim away from him, to change his path, to escape, but that immense mouth kept coming nearer and nearer.

"Hasten, Pinocchio, I beg you!" bleated the little Goat on the high rock.

And Pinocchio swam desperately with his arms, his body, his legs, his feet.

"Quick, Pinocchio, the monster is coming nearer!"

Pinocchio swam faster and faster, and harder and harder.

"Faster, Pinocchio! The monster will get you! There he is! There he is! Quick, quick, or you are lost!"

Pinocchio went through the water like a shot—swifter and swifter. He came close to the rock. The Goat leaned over and gave him one of her hoofs to help him up out of the water.

Alas! It was too late. The monster overtook him and the Marionette found himself in between the rows of gleaming white teeth. Only for a moment, however, for the Shark took a deep breath and, as he breathed, he drank in the Marionette as easily as he would have sucked an egg. Then he swallowed him so fast that Pinocchio, falling down into the body of the fish, lay stunned for a half-hour.

When he recovered his senses the Marionette could not remember where he was. Around him all was darkness, a darkness so deep and so black that for a moment he thought he had put his head into an inkwell. He listened for a few moments and heard nothing. Once in a while a cold wind blew on his face. At first he could not understand where that wind was coming from, but after a while he understood that it came from the lungs of the monster. I forgot to tell you that the Shark was suffering from asthma, so that whenever he breathed a storm seemed to blow.

Pinocchio at first tried to be brave, but as soon as he became convinced that he was really and truly in the Shark's stomach, he burst into sobs and tears. "Help! Help!" he cried. "Oh poor me! Won't someone come to save me?"

"Who is there to help you, unhappy boy?" said a rough voice, like a guitar out of tune.

"Who is talking?" asked Pinocchio, frozen with terror.

"It is I, a poor Tunny swallowed by the Shark at the same time as you. And what kind of a fish are you?"

"I have nothing to do with fishes. I am a Marionette."

"If you are not a fish, why did you let this monster swallow you?"

"I didn't let him. He chased me and swallowed me without even a 'by your leave'! And now what are we to do here in the dark?"

"Wait until the Shark has digested us both, I suppose."

"But I don't want to be digested," shouted Pinocchio, starting to sob.

"Neither do I," said the Tunny, "but I am wise enough to think that if one is born a fish, it is more dignified to die under the water than in the frying pan."

"What nonsense!" cried Pinocchio.

"Mine is an opinion," replied the Tunny, "and opinions should be respected."

"But I want to get out of this place. I want to escape."

"Go, if you can!"

"Is this Shark that has swallowed us very long?" asked the Marionette.

"His body, not counting the tail, is almost a mile long."

While talking in the darkness, Pinocchio thought he saw a faint light in the distance.

"What can that be?" he said to the Tunny.

"Some other poor fish, waiting as patiently as we to be digested by the Shark."

"I want to see him. He may be an old fish and may know some way of escape."

"I wish you all good luck, dear Marionette."

"Good-by, Tunny."

"Good-by, Marionette, and good luck."

"When shall I see you again?"

"Who knows? It is better not to think about it."

CHAPTER 35

In the Shark's body Pin-occhio finds whom? Read this chapter, my children, and you will know.

Pinocchio, as soon as he had said good-by to his good friend, the Tunny, tottered away in the darkness and began to walk as well as he could toward the faint light which glowed in the distance.

As he walked his feet splashed in a pool of greasy and slippery water, which had such a heavy smell of fish fried in oil that Pinocchio thought it was Lent.

The farther on he went, the brighter and clearer grew the tiny light. On and on he walked till finally he found—I give you a thousand guesses, my dear children! He found a little table set for dinner and lighted by a candle stuck in a glass bottle; and near the table sat a little old man, white as the snow, eating live fish.

They wriggled so that, now and again, one of them slipped out of the old man's mouth and escaped into the darkness under the table.

At this sight, the poor Marionette was filled with such great and sudden happiness that he almost dropped in a faint. He wanted to laugh, he wanted to cry, he wanted to say a thousand and one things, but all he could do was to stand still, stuttering and stammering brokenly. At last, with a great effort, he was able to let out a scream of joy and, opening wide his arms, he threw them around the old man's neck.

"Oh, Father, dear Father! Have I found you at last? Now I shall never, never leave you again!"

"Are my eyes really telling me the truth?" answered the old man, rubbing his eyes. "Are you really my own dear Pinocchio?"

"Yes, yes, yes! It is I! Look at me! And you have forgiven me, haven't you? Oh, my dear Father, how good you are! And to think that I—Oh, but if you only knew how many misfortunes have fallen on my head and how many troubles I have had! Just think that on the day you sold your old coat to buy me my A-B-C book so that I could go to school, I ran away to the Marionette Theater and the proprietor caught me and wanted to burn me to cook his roast lamb! He was the one who gave me the five gold pieces for you, but I met the Fox and the Cat, who took me to the Inn of the Red Lobster. There they ate like wolves and I left the Inn alone and I met the Assassins in the wood. I ran and they ran after me, always after me, till they hanged me to the branch of a giant oak tree. Then the Fairy of the Azure Hair sent the coach to rescue me and the doctors, after looking at me, said, 'If he is not dead, then he is surely alive,' and then I told a lie and my nose began to grow. It grew and it grew, till I couldn't get it through the door of the room. And then I went with the Fox and the Cat to the Field of Wonders to bury the gold pieces. The Parrot laughed at me and, instead of two thousand gold pieces, I found none. When the Judge heard I had been robbed, he sent me to jail to make the thieves happy; and when I came away I saw a fine bunch of grapes hanging on a vine. The trap caught me and the Farmer put a collar on me and made me a watchdog. He found out I was innocent when I caught the Weasels and

he let me go. The Serpent with the tail that smoked started to laugh and a vein in his chest broke and so I went back to the Fairy's house. She was dead, and the pigeon, seeing me crying, said to me, 'I have seen your father building a boat to look for you in America,' and I said to him, 'Oh, if I only had wings!' and he said to me, 'Do you want to go to your father?' and I said, 'Perhaps, but how?' and he said, 'Get on my back. I'll take you there.' We flew all night long, and the next morning the fishermen were looking toward the sea, crying, 'There is a poor little man drowning,' and I knew it was you, because my heart told me so, and I waved to you from the shore—"

"I knew you also," put in Geppetto, "and I wanted to go to you; but how could I? The sea was rough and the whitecaps overturned the boat. Then a Terrible Shark came up out of the sea and, as soon as he saw me in the water, swam quickly toward me, put out his tongue, and swallowed me as easily as if I had been a chocolate peppermint."

"And how long have you been shut away in here?"

"From that day to this, two long weary years—two years, my Pinocchio, which have been like two centuries."

"And how have you lived? Where did you find the candle? And the matches with which to light it—where did you get them?"

"You must know that, in the storm which swamped my boat, a large ship also suffered the same fate. The sailors were all saved, but the ship went right to the bottom of the sea, and the same Terrible Shark that swallowed me, swallowed most of it."

"What! Swallowed a ship?" asked Pinocchio in astonishment.

"At one gulp. The only thing he spat out was the mainmast, for it stuck in his teeth. To my own good luck, that ship was loaded with meat, preserved foods, crackers, bread, bottles of wine, raisins, cheese, coffee, sugar, wax candles, and boxes of matches. With all these blessings, I have been able to live happily on for two whole years, but now I am at the very last crumbs. Today there is nothing left in the cupboard, and this candle you see here is the last one I have."

"And then?"

"And then, my dear, we'll find ourselves in darkness."

"Then, my dear Father," said Pinocchio, "there is no time to lose. We must escape."

"Escape! How?"

"We can run out of the Shark's mouth and dive into the sea."

"You speak well, but I cannot swim, my dear Pinocchio."

"Why should that matter? You can climb on my shoulders and I, who am a fine swimmer, will carry you safely to the shore."

"Dreams, my boy!" answered Geppetto, shaking his head and smiling sadly. "Do you think it possible for a Marionette, a yard high, to have the strength to carry me on his shoulders and swim?"

"Try it and see! And in any case, if it is written that we must die, we shall at least die together."

Not adding another word, Pinocchio took the candle in his hand and going ahead to light the way, he said to his father:

"Follow me and have no fear."

They walked a long distance through the stomach and the whole body of the Shark. When they reached the throat of the monster, they stopped for a while to wait for the right moment in which to make their escape.

I want you to know that the Shark, being very old and suffering from asthma and heart trouble, was obliged to sleep with his mouth open. Because of this, Pinocchio was able to catch a glimpse of the sky filled with stars, as he looked up through the open jaws of his new home.

"The time has come for us to escape," he whispered, turning to his father. "The Shark is fast asleep. The sea is calm and the

night is as bright as day. Follow me closely, dear Father, and we shall soon be saved."

No sooner said than done. They climbed up the throat of the monster till they came to that immense open mouth. There they had to walk on tiptoes, for if they tickled the Shark's long tongue he might awaken—and where would they be then? The tongue was so wide and so long that it looked like a country road. The two fugitives were just about to dive into the sea when the Shark sneezed very suddenly and, as he sneezed, he gave Pinocchio and Geppetto such a jolt that they found themselves thrown on their backs and dashed once more and very unceremoniously into the stomach of the monster.

To make matters worse, the candle went out and father and son were left in the dark.

"And now?" asked Pinocchio with a serious face.

"Now we are lost."

"Why lost? Give me your hand, dear Father, and be careful not to slip!"

"Where will you take me?"

"We must try again. Come with me and don't be afraid."

With these words Pinocchio took his father by the hand and, always walking on tiptoes, they climbed up the monster's throat for a second time. They then crossed the whole tongue and jumped over three rows of teeth. But before they took the last great leap, the Marionette said to his father:

"Climb on my back and hold on tightly to my neck. I'll take care of everything else."

As soon as Geppetto was comfortably seated on his shoulders, Pinocchio, very sure of what he was doing, dived into the water and started to swim. The sea was like oil, the moon shone in all splendor, and the Shark continued to sleep so soundly that not even a cannon shot would have awakened him.

CHAPTER 36

Pinocchio finally ceases to be a Marionette and becomes a boy.

"My dear Father, we are saved!" cried the Marionette. "All we have to do now is to get to the shore, and that is easy."

Without another word, he swam swiftly away in an effort to reach land as soon as possible. All at once he noticed that Geppetto was shivering and shaking as if with a high fever.

Was he shivering from fear or from cold? Who knows? Perhaps a little of both. But Pinocchio, thinking his father was frightened, tried to comfort him by saying:

"Courage, Father! In a few moments we shall be safe on land."

"But where is that blessed shore?" asked the little old man, more and more worried as he tried to pierce the faraway shadows. "Here I am searching on all sides and I see nothing but sea and sky."

"I see the shore," said the Marionette. "Remember, Father, that I am like a cat. I see better at night than by day."

297

Poor Pinocchio pretended to be peaceful and contented, but he was far from that. He was beginning to feel discouraged, his strength was leaving him, and his breathing was becoming more and more labored. He felt he could not go on much longer, and the shore was still far away.

He swam a few more strokes. Then he turned to Geppetto and cried out weakly:

"Help me, Father! Help, for I am dying!"

Father and son were really about to drown when they heard a voice like a guitar out of tune call from the sea:

"What is the trouble?"

"It is I and my poor father."

"I know the voice. You are Pinocchio."

"Exactly. And you?"

"I am the Tunny, your companion in the Shark's stomach."

"And how did you escape?"

"I imitated your example. You are the one who showed me the way and after you went, I followed."

"Tunny, you arrived at the right moment! I implore you, for the love you bear your children, the little Tunnies, to help us, or we are lost!"

"With great pleasure indeed. Hang onto my tail, both of you, and let me lead you. In a twinkling you will be safe on land."

Geppetto and Pinocchio, as you can easily imagine, did not refuse the invitation; indeed, instead of hanging onto the tail, they thought it better to climb on the Tunny's back.

"Are we too heavy?" asked Pinocchio.

"Heavy? Not in the least. You are as light as sea shells," answered the Tunny, who was as large as a two-year-old horse.

As soon as they reached the shore, Pinocchio was the first to jump to the ground to help his old father. Then he turned to the fish and said to him:

"Dear friend, you have saved my father, and I have not enough words with which to thank you! Allow me to embrace you as a sign of my eternal gratitude."

The Tunny stuck his nose out of the water and Pinocchio knelt on the sand and kissed him most affectionately on his cheek. At this warm greeting, the poor Tunny, who was not used to such tenderness, wept like a child. He felt so embarrassed and ashamed that he turned quickly, plunged into the sea, and disappeared.

In the meantime day had dawned.

Pinocchio offered his arm to Geppetto, who was so weak he could hardly stand, and said to him:

"Lean on my arm, dear Father, and let us go. We will walk very, very slowly, and if we feel tired we can rest by the wayside."

"And where are we going?" asked Geppetto.

"To look for a house or a hut, where they will be kind enough to give us a bite of bread and a bit of straw to sleep on."

They had not taken a hundred steps when they saw two rough-looking individuals sitting on a stone begging for alms.

It was the Fox and the Cat, but one could hardly recognize them, they looked so miserable. The Cat, after pretending to be blind for so many years, had really lost the sight of both eyes. And the Fox, old, thin, and almost hairless, had even lost his tail.

That sly thief had fallen into deepest poverty, and one day he had been forced to sell his beautiful tail for a bite to eat.

"Oh, Pinocchio," he cried in a tearful voice. "Give us some alms, we beg of you! We are old, tired, and sick."

"Sick!" repeated the Cat.

"Addio, false friends!" answered the Marionette. "You cheated me once, but you will never catch me again."

"Believe us! Today we are truly poor and starving."

"Starving!" repeated the Cat.

"If you are poor, you deserve it! Remember the old proverb which says: 'Stolen money never bears fruit.' Addio, false friends."

"Have mercy on us!"

"On us."

"Addio, false friends. Remember the old proverb which says: 'Bad wheat always makes poor bread.'"

"Do not abandon us."

"Abandon us," repeated the Cat.

"Addio, false friends. Remember the old proverb: 'Whoever steals his neighbor's shirt, usually dies without his own.'"

Waving good-by to them, Pinocchio and Geppetto calmly went on their way. After a few more steps, they saw, at the end of a long road near a clump of trees, a tiny cottage built of straw.

"Someone must live in that little hut," said Pinocchio. "Let us see for ourselves."

They went and knocked at the door.

"Who is it?" said a little voice from within.

"A poor father and a poorer son, without food and with no roof to cover them" answered the Marionette.

"Turn the key and the door will open," said the same little voice.

Pinocchio turned the key and the door opened. As soon as they went in, they looked here and there and everywhere but saw no one.

"Oh—ho, where is the owner of the hut?" cried Pinocchio, very much surprised.

"Here I am, up here!"

Father and son looked up to the ceiling, and there on a beam sat the Talking Cricket.

"Oh, my dear Cricket," said Pinocchio, bowing politely.

"Oh, now you call me your dear Cricket, but do you remember when you threw your hammer at me to kill me?"

"You are right, dear Cricket. Throw a hammer at me now. I deserve it! But spare my poor old father."

"I am going to spare both the father and the son. I have only wanted to remind you of the trick you long ago played upon me, to teach you that in this world of ours we must be kind and courteous to others, if we want to find kindness and courtesy in our own days of trouble."

"You are right, little Cricket, you are more than right, and I shall remember the lesson you have taught me. But will you tell how you succeeded in buying this pretty little cottage?"

"This cottage was given to me yesterday by a little Goat with blue hair."

"And where did the Goat go?" asked Pinocchio.

"I don't know."

"And when will she come back?"

"She will never come back. Yesterday she went away bleating sadly, and it seemed to me she said: 'Poor Pinocchio, I shall never see him again . . . the Shark must have eaten him by this time.' "

"Were those her real words? Then it was she—it was—my dear little Fairy," cried out Pinocchio, sobbing bitterly.

After he had cried a long time, he wiped his eyes and then he made a bed of straw for old Geppetto. He laid him on it and said to the Talking Cricket:

"Tell me, little Cricket, where shall I find a glass of milk for my poor Father?"

"Three fields away from here lives Farmer John. He has some cows. Go there and he will give you what you want."

Pinocchio ran all the way to Farmer John's house. The Farmer said to him:

"How much milk do you want?"

"I want a full glass."

"A full glass costs a penny. First give me the penny."

"I have no penny," answered Pinocchio, sad and ashamed.

"Very bad, my Marionette," answered the Farmer, "very bad. If you have no penny, I have no milk."

"Too bad," said Pinocchio and started to go.

"Wait a moment," said Farmer John. "Perhaps we can come to terms. Do you know how to draw water from a well?"

"I can try."

"Then go to that well you see yonder and draw one hundred bucketfuls of water."

"Very well."

"After you have finished, I shall give you a glass of warm sweet milk."

"I am satisfied."

Farmer John took the Marionette to the well and showed him how to draw the water. Pinocchio set to work as well as he knew how, but long before he had pulled up the one hundred buckets, he was tired out and dripping with perspiration. He had never worked so hard in his life.

"Until today," said the Farmer, "my donkey has drawn the water for me, but now that poor animal is dying."

"Will you take me to see him?" said Pinocchio.

"Gladly."

As soon as Pinocchio went into the stable, he spied a little Donkey lying on a bed of straw in the corner of the stable. He was worn out from hunger and too much work. After looking at him a long time, Pinocchio said to himself: "I know that Donkey! I have seen him before." Bending low over him, he asked: "Who are you?"

At this question, the Donkey opened weary, dying eyes and answered in the same tongue: "I am Lamp-Wick."

Then he closed his eyes and died.

"Oh, my poor Lamp-Wick," said Pinocchio in a faint voice, as he wiped his eyes with some straw he had picked up from the ground.

"Do you feel so sorry for a little donkey that has cost you nothing?" said the Farmer. "What should I do—I, who have paid my good money for him?"

"But, you see, he was my friend."

"Your friend?"

"A classmate of mine."

"What," shouted Farmer John, bursting out laughing. "What! You had donkeys in your school? How you must have studied!"

The Marionette, ashamed and hurt by those words, did not answer, but taking his glass of milk returned to his father.

From that day on, for more than five months, Pinocchio got up every morning just as dawn was breaking and went to the farm to draw water. And every day he was given a glass of warm milk for his poor old father, who grew stronger and better day by day. But he was not satisfied with this. He learned to make baskets of reeds and sold them. With the money he received, he and his father were able to keep from starving.

Among other things, he built a rolling chair, strong and comfortable, to take his old father out for an airing on bright, sunny days.

In the evening the Marionette studied by lamplight. With some of the money he had earned, he bought himself a second-hand volume that had a few pages missing, and with that he learned to read in a very short time. As far as writing was concerned, he used a long stick at one end of which he had whittled a long, fine point. Ink he had none, so he used the juice of blackberries or cherries.

Little by little his diligence was rewarded. He succeeded, not only in his studies, but also in his work, and a day came when he put enough money together to keep his old father comfortable and happy. Besides this, he was able to save the great amount of fifty pennies. With it he wanted to buy himself a new suit.

One day he said to his father:

"I am going to the market place to buy myself a coat, a cap, and a pair of shoes. When I come back I'll be so dressed up, you will think I am a rich man."

He ran out of the house and up the road to the village, laughing and singing. Suddenly he heard his name called, and looking around to see whence the voice came, he noticed a large snail crawling out of some bushes.

"Don't you recognize me?" said the Snail.

"Yes and no."

"Do you remember the Snail that lived with the Fairy with Azure Hair? Do you not remember how she opened the door for you one night and gave you something to eat?"

"I remember everything," cried Pinocchio. "Answer me quickly, pretty Snail, where have you left my Fairy? What is she doing? Has she forgiven me? Does she remember me? Does she still love me? Is she very far away from here? May I see her?"

At all these questions, tumbling out one after another, the Snail answered, calm as ever:

"My dear Pinocchio, the Fairy is lying ill in a hospital."

"In a hospital?"

"Yes, indeed. She has been stricken with trouble and illness, and she hasn't a penny left with which to buy a bite of bread."

"Really? Oh, how sorry I am! My poor, dear little Fairy! If I had a million I should run to her with it! But I have only fifty pennies. Here they are. I was just going to buy some clothes. Here, take them, little Snail, and give them to my good Fairy."

"What about the new clothes?"

"What does that matter? I should like to sell these rags I have on to help her more. Go, and hurry. Come back here within a couple of days and I hope to have more money for you! Until to-day I have worked for my father. Now I shall have to work for my mother also. Good-by, and I hope to see you soon."

The Snail, much against her usual habit, began to run like a lizard under a summer sun.

When Pinocchio returned home, his father asked him:

"And where is the new suit?"

"I couldn't find one to fit me. I shall have to look again some other day."

That night Pinocchio, instead of going to bed at ten o'clock, waited until midnight, and instead of making eight baskets, he made sixteen.

After that he went to bed and fell asleep. As he slept, he dreamed of his Fairy, beautiful, smiling, and happy, who kissed him and said to him: "Bravo, Pinocchio! In reward for your kind heart, I forgive you for all your old mischief. Boys who love and take good care of their parents when they are old and sick, deserve praise even though they may not be held up as models of obedience and good behavior. Keep on doing so well, and you will be happy."

At that very moment, Pinocchio awoke and opened wide his eyes.

What was his surprise and his joy when, on looking himself over, he saw that he was no longer a Marionette, but that he had become a real live boy! He looked all about him and instead of the usual walls of straw, he found himself in a beautifully furnished little room, the prettiest he had ever seen. In a twinkling, he jumped down from his bed to look on the chair standing near. There he found a new suit, a new hat, and a pair of shoes.

As soon as he was dressed, he put his hands in his pockets and pulled out a little leather purse on which were written the following words: "The Fairy with Azure Hair returns fifty pennies to her dear Pinocchio with many thanks for his kind heart." The Marionette opened the purse to find the money, and behold— there were fifty gold coins!

Pinocchio ran to the mirror. He hardly recognized himself. The bright face of a tall boy looked at him with wide-awake blue eyes, dark brown hair and happy, smiling lips.

Surrounded by so much splendor, the Marionette hardly knew what he was doing. He rubbed his eyes two or three times, wondering if he were still asleep or awake and decided he must be awake.

"And where is Father?" he cried suddenly. He ran into the next room, and there stood Geppetto, grown years younger overnight, spick and span in his new clothes and gay as a lark in the morning. He was once more Mastro Geppetto, the wood carver, hard at work on a lovely picture frame, decorating it with flowers and leaves, and heads of animals.

"Father, Father, what has happened? Tell me if you can," cried Pinocchio, as he ran and jumped on his Father's neck.

"This sudden change in our house is all your doing, my dear Pinocchio," answered Geppetto.

"What have I to do with it?"

"Just this. When bad boys become good and kind, they have the power of making their homes gay and new with happiness."

"I wonder where the old Pinocchio of wood has hidden himself?"

"There he is," answered Geppetto. And he pointed to a large Marionette leaning against a chair, head turned to one side, arms hanging limp, and legs twisted under him.

After a long, long look, Pinocchio said to himself with great content:

"How ridiculous I was as a Marionette! And how happy I am, now that I have become a real boy!"